DREAMWEAVERS

Patricia M. Robertson

*"My theory . . . is that with things and places,
and possibly with people too,
it's easier to let them go when you must,
if you have let yourself love them, than if you've held back."*

Mary Morrison, *Let Evening Come*

I

Kate watched her sixteen-year-old daughter walk through airport security and down the terminal, off to new adventures, a summer in California with her dad and step-mom. She stood long after her daughter had disappeared out of sight. It would be a long summer. How would she survive?

"Get a life," Terri had snapped at her as Kate had followed her from room to room like a puppy dog while she was packing.

"I have a life," Kate defended herself. "I have my work, my home, my friends, and you."

"You don't have me, Mom. Get that into your head. If you have a life, then why have you been following me everywhere this week? If the bathroom door didn't have a lock, I bet you would have followed me there."

"I just wanted to make the most of this last week before you left."

"I'm not moving away forever. Just for the summer. I'll be back before you even have time to miss me."

Fat chance of that, Kate thought to herself. I miss her already. There was an emptiness inside her, an emptiness that used to be filled by her little girl. Now she was no longer her little girl.

"Hi, Scott," Kate said to the radio announcer as she listened during the drive home. She missed Terri telling her to cut it out. Kate didn't understand why Terri thought it was so weird that she liked to talk to the radio.

Terri also didn't understand why Kate talked back to those inane recordings on the phone.

"I want to talk to a real person. Could I please talk to a real person? Is there any such thing as a live person that I can talk to?"

"Mom, what are you doing?"

"I've been on hold for ten minutes. I've been given twenty different options for recordings but no option to talk to a real person. What do you think I'm doing?"

"Gee, calm down, Mom, it's just a phone."

"Just a phone! No, I don't want to hear the menu again. Can I please talk to a real person?"

Terri walked away shaking her head.

"You try it. Just wait till you get stuck on hold just to straighten out a simple problem on your bill. Just wait till you have to go through countless menus of options, none of which includes the problem you are dealing with. You'll change your tune," Kate had shouted after her.

Terri couldn't understand why she talked to the voices from the radio. Kate didn't see what the big deal was. It's not as if they ever answered her back. It's not as if they heard her. It was fun to carry on this conversation with the radio. She could say whatever she wanted. It was almost as if they were old friends. Same thing with the phone, although that was not as much fun. It was just an opportunity to let off some steam. No one was hurt by it. She didn't see why Terri had such a problem with it. She missed her already.

Premature empty nest syndrome, she told herself. She knew all about the empty nest syndrome. She had told herself it would not get to her. Not the way it got to some women. Not the way it had affected her mom. She had meaningful work, friends, her house. Certainly she had enough going on in her life to compensate for the loss of her role as the parent of a child still at home. She didn't have any love interest, but that would come with time, she had assured herself – when she actually had time for romance. Who had time for an active social life while single parenting, pursuing a Master's degree and working?

She thought she had been doing pretty good, considering. But now, faced with a summer alone she had felt tears near the surface for the last two months. It didn't make sense. It was too soon. And yet it did make sense. She cried as much at the graduation of friends' children this year as if it had been her daughter walking across that stage. Didn't make sense, and yet it made all the sense in the world. Maybe Terri was right. Maybe she did need to get a life.

She remembered another airplane – was it actually thirty years ago? Doesn't seem possible. Funny how each year her daughter ages, she finds memories she thought she had forgotten, or at least put aside for later, popping up. Guess now is later. Memories came from when she was her daughter's age; memories now seen in a new light after so many years.

She remembered standing at another airport, watching another plane, when she herself had been sixteen. This had been the end of the summer, not the beginning. She had been saying goodbye to the boy she had dated that summer, a summer romance, her first. She had wondered why she was even there. They hadn't known each other that long. But he had wanted her to come and so she had. Then she was left standing with his grandparents, leaving with them as she sat quietly in the back of the car for the long drive home.

Funny. He had said he would be back to visit. Of course he said that. Don't they all? Don't we all? We always say we'll be back, that we'll see each other again, and then what happens? Time slips by, days turn into weeks, weeks into months and years and before you know it, it's thirty years later and you are saying goodbye to your daughter as she embarks on an adventure that doesn't include you. She'll be back. This you can count on. She's flesh and blood, your daughter, unlike the men in your life. She'll be back.

She hit speed dial on her cell phone.

"She's gone."

"You okay? You want me to come over?" her sister responded.

"No, I'll be fine. I have to get used to an empty house. No sense in putting it off." Kate paused as she turned a corner, "Do you remember Frank Shaughnessy?"

"Didn't you date him for a while in high school? Why?"

"Just thinking about him for some reason. It's been thirty years since that summer. Doesn't seem possible. I wonder what happened to him."

"Why don't you Google him and see what you can find?"

"Google him? Sounds kind of kinky," Kate said with a smile.

"Everybody does it. Just enter his name in Google search and see what you can find."

"I don't know, I'll think about it," Kate said as she pulled into her driveway. "Gotta go. I'll call you tomorrow."

Funny. There was part of her that had known even then that he wouldn't be back, at least not next summer as he had said. Part of her believed it, wanted to believe, another part believed he would be back, but not for a long time. Not for many years. Funny how the heart works. We create fantasies, then hold onto them until they feel almost real. There was a part of her that never forgot; a part of her that was convinced they'd meet again, some future day, some future time.

Throughout the years, especially since her divorce, she had thought about looking him up. But it never seemed to be the right time. She was busy about so many things, busy putting her life back together, building a career, raising her daughter. Who had time for a social life or looking up lost boyfriends? And, if she had found him, what then? Chances were that he was married. It would have been interesting to know what he was doing, but not interesting enough to get her to actually make the effort. And now that she had the time, was it too late?

When you are young, time stretches before you like an endless supply, grains of sand in a desert or drops of water in the ocean. There will always be plenty of it, you think. And then you are forty-six and ever so much older than before. You realize that time is running out, has already run out on some of your dreams.

Terri's dog, Cookie, eagerly awaited their return. She ran from room to room when let in, a collie, beautiful, thoroughbred and a nuisance to brush, Kate thought as she refilled Cookie's water dish and poured food into her bowl. Yet Kate was glad for the company.

"You miss her too, don't you, old girl? Come on. For the summer it's just you and me."

Kate got out Cookie's leash and proceeded to take her on her daily walk. "Well, at least I won't lack for exercise this summer, between the dog and the lawn." Hers was a small yard, nestled snugly between the other houses in the block. Still, there was mowing and trimming bushes, pulling weeds out of the flower beds and out of cracks in the driveway and sidewalk. There was plenty to keep her busy. Jobs Terri used to help do.

She let Cookie off her leash as they approached the house, giving her a chance to run before coming in for the night. Cookie took off after a little prompting. She wasn't as fast as she used to be.

"Getting older, aren't we?" Kate commented as she patted Cookie and let her in. She remembered when she had brought Cookie home from the pet store. Terri had fallen in love at first sight. Kate had hoped to steer her towards a smaller dog, one with less hair, maybe a little easier to keep, but Terri had her heart set on a collie after having watched too many Lassie reruns on Nickelodeon. Cookie's fur had been the color of fresh-cooked peanut butter cookies, golden brown, Terri's favorite, hence the name.

"Oh, Cookie, I could eat you up," Terri had exclaimed when they finally got home with the dog and all of the other dog paraphernalia like a leash, a rope, a dog bowl, flea collar and dog food. That had been ten years ago. Cookie had proved herself well worth the hassle of house training and the expense of vet bills. Not only was she a great companion for Terri as she grew, but she also proved to be a good home-security system. Kate felt looked over and secure every time she heard the familiar sound of Cookie's nails on the hardwood floors in the bedrooms as Cookie made her rounds checking first on Terri, then on her and then the rest of the house before settling down on her pillow in Terri's room. Burglars beware, Kate had always thought once Cookie reached maturity. Well worth the investment.

Now she was slowing down, but she still was a deterrent to any who might want to break in. At least Kate felt more secure knowing she was here, as well as less lonely.

"Come on, girl," she said as she picked up the paper from the front porch and proceeded into the house.

Her dinner was a glass of wine and a bag of microwave popcorn. Not a good start to the summer, she told herself. Tomorrow she would do better, but she just didn't feel like cooking just for her. In fact, it felt good not to cook. There are worse things she could eat, like a bag of potato chips, finished off by ice cream and brownies. Hmm, ice cream, she thought to herself. She was pretty sure there was still some of Terri's favorite ice cream in the freezer. Tomorrow she would be better, she reassured herself as she finished off the carton of pistachio ice cream, eating directly from the carton and giving the remainder to Cookie.

"Just for today. Just a treat for today, Cookie. We two old women might as well have some fun," she told Cookie as she set the ice cream carton on the floor.

Maybe Terri was right, she thought to herself again. Maybe it was time to branch out a little, expand her horizon. She thought once more about Frank.

Franklin James Shaughnessy, Jr. She hadn't forgotten him completely. She had thought about doing a search on the Internet, but most of the services that would have found him for her had a charge. She hadn't been willing to pay, not then anyway. It was too weird, too scary. What if he found out she was looking for him? What would she find? It was one thing to casually look on the Internet. Then she could have said, "Oh, I had nothing better to do so I entered your name and found you." That was much better than spending money to look someone up. She wanted it casual, very casual. She had wanted to find a way to slip in, take a look at his life, see what he had done and what he was doing, see the man he had become, and then decide whether she wanted any further contact with him. And so she hadn't pursued it any further than that.

She poured herself a glass of wine, turned on her computer, entered her name and password and went to Google search. There weren't a lot of entries under his name, only a hundred or so. Not like some searches that brought up thousands. There he was, Franklin James Shaughnessy, but it looked like an obituary. She clicked on the site, heart in her throat, to see his name, but the date of birth was wrong, 1933. It couldn't have been her Frank. Must have been his dad. All of the other info fit. She tried to find more information, family, anything that would link this Frank with her Frank. His name had shown up on the West Point obituaries. To The Fallen, it had read.

She remembered he had been a Brigadier General, somehow associated with West Point. She didn't know much more than that. Frank had been a military brat, moving from one base to the next. He had envied her for having a stable home in the same town. She had reassured him it was nothing to be envious about. Morenci had been no great Mecca of excitement for teens. She couldn't wait to get out. But he had persisted. He had not been looking forward to his latest move, Fort Dix. That, as much as anything, had probably contributed to his wanting to stay in Morenci with his grandparents and her.

"But, why stay?" she had asked him.

"You just want me to say it," he had insisted.

"No, I don't. There is nothing here."

"You know why," he continued to insist and kissed her.

Because of me, she had thought with disbelief and dismay. You hardly know me and yet you're going to change your life because of me. That's crazy, don't be a fool. She had wanted to protest, yet he still didn't come right out and say it. Maybe she was wrong. What if she was wrong? What if she said it only to have him laugh at her presumptuousness?

She pulled away from his embrace, much as she was enjoying it.

"You still didn't tell me," she insisted.

"Because of you," he said and they kissed again. She allowed herself to sink into the kiss. Don't think, she had told herself. Just lose yourself in the kiss. Finally they said goodbye. She went into her home, walked to her room, shut her bedroom door and panicked.

Because of me? Because of me? What am I going to do? What if we have a fight? What if we break up and here he is stuck in Morenci for the rest of the year? Stuck in Morenci. He'll come to hate me for it. Kate had determined to dissuade him from such foolishness, only to find the problem had solved itself. The next day Frank told her his parents had not agreed to him staying and had insisted he join them. They had booked a flight for him for Saturday.

That problem had been solved. She had been relieved and saddened. It had never occurred to her how much she would miss him until he was gone. This was before the day of the Internet. They had to rely on snail mail and Frank had not been a faithful writer. The phone was expensive, besides the complete lack of privacy in her house. They only had the one phone in the kitchen. No cordless phone that could be taken to the privacy of your bedroom. And then there was the constant reminder by her mom not to tie up the phone too long in case someone needed to call her dad. Yes, the relationship had been doomed. Still she had held onto the hope of seeing him again.

"And now Terri is gone too," Kate said as she reached down and petted Cookie. "Why does everyone have to leave?"

She continued clicking on other sites trying to find more information. Two led right back to the first obituary. Then she found something useful: The Aviation News. There was something about a pilot, Lieutenant Frank J. Shaughnessy. She clicked on the site, waited for her slow connection to go through. When it finally completed, there he was, his picture looking back at her. She had gasped once again. It had to be him. She didn't have any picture of him. He had never sent her one, just as she had not sent him her picture. She had hated her senior picture and didn't want him to have it. She had wanted to find a better one to send him but didn't have any at the time.

This had to be him, handsome in his uniform. He must have been all of twenty-six when the picture was taken. He was smiling, not a toothy grin, but a military smile, as befitting an officer, short, sandy brown hair, blue-grey eyes. It was him. She paused and sipped her wine as she looked at the picture, transported back in time.

So, he, too, had gone into the military, Kate thought, like his dad, only he had been a pilot. She looked over the record below the picture. Nothing about him being married, nothing about kids— these military, they leave out all the important details. Nothing about whether he was happy. Instead it spoke of missions, flights, honors.

He had participated in Operation Desert Storm and had left active duty in 1985, the same year his dad had died. Obviously the two must be connected. Did he leave from grief over his dad's death? Maybe he had only gone into the military to please his dad and now that his dad was gone there was no longer any reason to stay. Maybe he was angry at the military for his dad's death. His father's obituary didn't say anything about dying in combat like others in the obituaries.

What did he do after that? Did he sink into depression, an early mid-life crisis? Maybe he became a commercial pilot and made lots of money to make up for years of military pay. Was he married? Did he have kids? Further searching revealed nothing more about Frank, although there was another Shaughnessy, Chad, that she found in the military. A younger one. Could he be a son to Frank, grandson to Frank Sr.? Or maybe a nephew. Frank had had a sister, but then his sister's last name wouldn't be Shaughnessy, but her married name. This younger Shaughnessy name came up under a eulogy for Frank Sr., commenting on how he had admired him and had heard so much about him, although he never knew him.

Further searching gave no more answers and certainly not the one she most wanted to know: How was Frank now? What was he doing? If he had married, which she figured was so, was he still married? Did he ever give a thought to her?

And what about her other friends from high school? She wondered what they were doing, how they were doing. Over the years she had lost touch with all of them. Her parents still lived in her hometown, in the same house they had lived in for the last fifty years. Kate visited them, but for the most part she had wanted to get out of her hometown once she graduated from high school. She had never looked back.

She had considered attending her twenty-fifth reunion, but she had no idea who would show up since she had lost all contact with her former friends. She was afraid of showing up and seeing a room full of strangers. Something that was quite possible when you figure there were about three hundred in her graduating class. There were a number of students who went through all four years with her whom she had never actually met, much less gotten to know. No, she figured, the party can go on without her. Still, if only there were some way she could find out what her old friends were doing.

She put down her wine and started another search to see what she could find. While not exactly a novice on the computer, she was certainly no computer geek. She had yet to learn the intricacies of chat rooms, although she had talked Terri into giving her a brief intro before she left. Kate figured this would probably be her best bet at communicating with Terri over the summer. Perhaps she would get a phone call. Terri certainly wouldn't write, but she definitely would not spend two months away from friends without contacting them via computer. Kate figured the best way to contact

Terri would be email or instant messenger, if she could remember how it's done.

She sent a hasty email to Terri asking her how her trip was and assuring her that she was taking care of Cookie. Then she went to google.com to do a search. She tried the names for some of her former classmates but had no luck. Either there were so many entries she couldn't begin to narrow it down, or there were no entries. She entered Shaughnessy, Franklin James again. The same hundred entries came up; nothing new from the last time she had tried the search. She clicked again on the ones she had found to have helpful information. First, Frank's dad's obituary, nothing new there. Then she clicked on the Aviation news and Frank's picture.

She wondered what he had looked like as he got older. Had he grown bald and with a pot-belly? She doubted the pot-belly, given how concerned Frank had been about his build at seventeen. Still, you never knew what the years can do to a person. It was weird to think of him in the military, especially with the troubles in the Middle East. Had he been involved in all of that? The article had said he had served in Desert Storm. How long was he there? Was his son in the Middle East now, if that was his son? Had he ever been called back into service? It made the war so much more real and personal thinking someone she had once cared for had been serving in the Middle East.

She pulled herself away from the computer and finished off her wine. It had been a long day, time to go to sleep. She lay down but her mind gave her little rest. She kept thinking of that picture. What-ifs filled her mind. What if they had stayed together? What if they had continued to date through college? What if they had married? What a thought, married to a fighter pilot. She who, in her twenties, had been arrested at Air Force bases protesting the Nuclear weapons build-up and cruise missiles. What if he had been stationed at one of those bases? Certainly he would not have recognized her among all of those peace nuts. He probably would have just driven by without looking at them, ignoring them and their signs.

Or maybe he was one of the ones who had yelled at them, "Nuke them till they glow, then shoot them in the dark. Let God sort them out." She and her friends had found that quite comical

10

and had had a good laugh over it later that day when gathered at a local church recounting the day's activities and planning for the next day. Still, what a jerk if that had been him. She found herself getting angry with him just thinking about it.

There's no way she could have married someone in the military. No way. She could go out with someone whose dad was a general because, after all, we can't help who our parents are. But a soldier himself, no way! Although he was cute in uniform.

What am I thinking, she chided herself. Still the fantasy had a life of its own. She could see him arresting her along with the others, not recognizing who she was until she turned to face him. Then there would have been a moment of recognition and embarrassment as they stumbled over what to say.

"Kate?"

"Frank?"

"What are you doing here?" they would both ask in unison, then laugh. "It's obvious, isn't it?" again in unison.

Her current boyfriend steps forward in her imagination, "We're here to make a statement. To ask you to stop participating in using these weapons of mass destruction."

"Yeah, yeah, somebody handcuff this guy and get him on the bus." Two other MP's drag Dick away while Kate remains there, sure she is seeing an illusion.

"So, what are you doing here?" Frank asked again.

"Well, it's kind of like he said."

"You're one of them."

"What do you mean, one of them? If you mean somebody who cares about this world and not destroying it, leaving it a better place for future generations, then I'm one of them."

"No, you're not, Katy. They're a bunch of kooks."

"I think you better arrest me so I can take my place on the bus with the other kooks."

"Hey, Sarge, what's the hold-up?" one of the MP's called over to Frank.

"Suit yourself," Frank said and walked away as they handcuffed Kate.

"Who was that?" Dick asked when she joined him on the bus for the ride to jail.

"Just someone I thought I knew," Kate remarked. It became so real in her head she almost believed it had happened. Jerk, she thought. Of course they would have fought. The two of them – just a disaster in the making. It never would have worked out. She was better off the way it had ended, better off without him. Of course, her marriage had been a disaster as well, but that disaster had yielded her a daughter.

Kate finally drifted off to sleep. In her dreams she was in her twenties again, a flower child putting a daisy in the end of Frank's gun as he stared straight ahead, pretending not to recognize her, like the guards at Buckingham Palace. Then she was putting flowers on his grave. She woke up with a start, reminded herself it was a dream and attempted to return to sleep.

"Hi, Terri," Terri was relieved to see her dad waiting for her at the airport baggage. Relieved to see it was just him, wife nowhere in sight. She was both relieved and anxious. It was good to think she would have some time with her dad by herself before getting to what would be her home for the summer. And she was anxious because she had no idea what they would talk about during the car ride.

She resented being dragged across the country away from her friends for the summer, resented the thought of being stuck with her stepbrother and stepsister all summer. She feared she would end up being a free babysitting service all summer. Nothing had been said about it. She was afraid it would just be presumed. Whenever she had stayed at her dad's before, she had had to share a room with her stepsister, Alyssa. She dreaded a summer of this. Still it was California. It was an opportunity to get away from small-town Midwestern life for the West Coast. Maybe it wouldn't be so bad. She could have insisted on staying home for the summer. She was old enough to make her own decision on this. She had decided to give it a try.

"Hey, Dad," she greeted him with a hug. "Where's Janet?"

"Oh, the kids got restless – so she took them outside for a while. Not much to do at an airport since the stepped-up security. Can't even watch planes take off and land. It probably wasn't a good idea bringing them, but they were excited about having a big sister for the summer. They didn't want to stay home."

"Oh," Terri replied, trying to mask her feelings, this time relief mixed with disappointment. Oh, well, she'd have all summer to spend time with him. Maybe, sometime, maybe there will be time. Maybe it will be like it was before he remarried, when he would spend time with her, just her.

"Here they are," her dad said as her stepmother arrived, preceded by her eight-year-old stepbrother, Alex, and six-year-old stepsister, Alyssa.

"Terri!" they squealed and ran to give her hugs. It was nice to see them so genuinely happy to see her. Her stepmother smiled warmly, too. She had wondered what her stepmother had thought about having the added responsibility of a teenager this summer, but she seemed genuinely okay with it. Terri experienced more relief, minus the anxiety and disappointment.

"I've arranged for you to work at the local country club," her dad told her during the drive to their home. "Hope you don't mind. It's only bussing tables, but it will give you a chance to meet people and make a little spending money."

"That's fine, but what about the kids?"

"We couldn't expect you to spend your summer vacation babysitting. They'll be going to day camp most days," her stepmom chimed in.

Terri was surprised when they pulled up in front of a large, sprawling house complete with pool, twice the size of their house at home. It must be true, she thought, how they say every house in California has a pool. She was doubly surprised when they showed her to her own room, complete with bathroom.

"You mean I don't have to share with Alyssa?"

"Didn't your father tell you?" Janet asked. "How like a man to forget something so important. Actually this is the guest room, but now that you are here, it is your room. Like it?"

"It's great," Terri said, dropping onto the bed. She was finding it hard to maintain her original resentment about the move and the summer. It might not be so bad after all. She didn't know about bussing dishes at the country club, but it would be nice to have some spending money.

"Won't you get lonely all by yourself in this room?" Alyssa asked.

"If I do, I know just where to look for you," Terri said, giving Alyssa a hug.

Sunday morning. Kate didn't want to get out of bed. What reason did she have to get out of bed, she wondered? She had the whole day ahead of her, plenty of time to brood. She could go to church. Maybe that would take her mind off of Terri, maybe not. At least it would help pass some of the time.

She attended the service, but her mind was somewhere else. When she got home she decided to check her email just in case Terri had sent something. Sure enough, there was one message waiting. "Arrived here safely. Flight was fine. Give Cookie a hug for me. Don't give her too many treats while I'm gone. Love, Terri."

It wasn't much, but it was contact. Since the computer was on and she had time on her hands, she decided to go back to the website with Frank's picture. She wasn't sure why. She just wanted to see it. That's probably how he looked back when I was getting busted at Air Force bases, she thought. She went back over the items from her search hoping to find something she had missed. Nothing new. She wondered how often they updated their website, if they ever did. Finally she shut the computer off.

II

Kate was grateful to get back to work the next day. She needed something to get her mind off Terri – that is, something besides Frank. Work was just the ticket, or her other children, as Terri termed them. Kate worked with pregnant teens. The idea was to break the cycle of poverty and abuse by helping these young women, teaching them parenting skills they had never learned from their own parents, helping them stay in school, develop job skills and life skills necessary to make it in the world.

"Good morning, Ms. Connors."

"Monique, I thought you had summer school today. What are you doing still here?"

"Tanya's sick. She didn't want me to leave her." Kate looked at Monique, her swollen belly and the child of eighteen months, sniffling on her hip, and shook her head.

"I'll talk to you later," she said as she went to her office.

It was fulfilling work, if somewhat frustrating. There were success stories, as well as relapses when these young women, back in their home environments, ended up pregnant again, back with an old boyfriend and out of school. Still, the successes outweighed the failures. She was able to take these young women who came at a vulnerable time in their lives, many having been abused themselves as children, and help them in ways she wasn't able to help her own daughter.

Not that Terri had the problems these girls did. Quite the contrary. Still, sometimes she had breakthroughs with these girls; sometimes they listened to her more than her own daughter who had heard all she had to say many times over, or so Terri thought, and who needed to break away, become her own person, separate from her mom.

Kate understood the dynamics all too well. She hadn't spent all those years getting her MSW for nothing. It still didn't make it any easier where her daughter was concerned. It was a nice escape into another reality, working with the girls at the shelter, especially when she was able to steer clear of all the supposedly necessary paperwork that took her away from contact hours with the girls, paperwork like the piles that greeted her on her return to her office that morning. She had cleared away her schedule in order to finally tackle the mounds of paperwork she had backlogged. She was so busy, finally making some headway to being able to see the top of her desk, that she almost forgot she was supposed to meet the contractor at her house over her lunch hour to finalize the work that was to be done over the summer.

Kate reluctantly put aside the remaining case files, hoping to get to them that afternoon, between group sessions and appointments, and hurried out the door, pulling up at her home at the same time as the contractor.

"Right on time," he smiled as he got out of his truck and sauntered towards her.

"Well, almost," she said realizing that she was ten minutes late, as she parked her car.

"Right on time according to my time frame," he smiled again.

"That's probably true," Kate commented. Had she ever dealt with anyone in construction that did anything "on time"? Normally, it was – they'll come sometime between nine and twelve – and then after you've missed a whole morning of work you call to find out they are behind schedule and either will have to reschedule or come at one, meaning you were now out a whole day of work.

"How about I subtract from your bill the hours I lost from work waiting for you," Kate had commented to a plumber once.

"Look, lady, if you don't want me to do the job, I've got other work to do," was the usual response. And so you were at their mercy.

This man was unusually prompt, although they were still finalizing the deal. She found contractors were always very good about returning calls and keeping appointments when you were working out whether they had the job or not. The minute you signed the agreement you were back on their time.

Kate had decided to do some major remodeling while Terri was gone. Changes she had wanted to do for some time now but had been putting off. Now seemed like the perfect time. She was done paying off her own college loans and had two years before

Terri would be in college. Time to do the changes she had wanted for so long. Theirs was a simple, two-story home, three bedrooms, one bath. She had been using the third bedroom as a home office but was willing to give it up for a second bath. What a luxury not to have to trip over the steps going downstairs at night when nature called.

She was remodeling the kitchen, adding a breakfast nook where she could sit and have coffee on cold winter mornings while enjoying a clear view on three sides of the outdoors. It would also be a cozy and convenient place for meals. Their dining room had long been overrun by the computer and would double nicely as an office to replace the one she was losing. What did they need a dining room for anyway with just the two of them – and eventually just her? The table could always be brought out and expanded if needed for entertaining guests, but that happened so rarely it seemed like an unnecessary waste of space. As it was, the table, pushed into one corner, doubled as extra workspace, giving Terri room to sprawl out whatever homework projects she was working on and overflow space for other books, papers, magazines.

A breakfast nook would suit them just fine for the vast majority of their dining needs. She could hardly remember the last time they had actually used the dining room table for a meal together. Maybe it had been Christmas or Easter. Often they piled food on their plates, then sat in the living room, watching Simpson reruns to break up the monotony of the day.

It hadn't always been like this. There had been a time, not so long ago, when they had had real meals at the table together, back when Terri's dad had still been there, but even since then. She wasn't sure how what had been an occasional treat, eating dinner in front of the TV, had turned into their routine, but maybe now was her chance to change this. One last effort, anyway, before Terri moved out. Even if it didn't manage to change that habit, at least she would have her breakfast nook, something she'd wanted for a long time.

The downstairs bathroom was going to be expanded to make space for a utility room for her washer and dryer. This would save countless steps and simplify her life so much. No more running down those rickety stairs to the basement to do laundry, straining at the top of the steps to see if she could hear whether the dryer was still running; running up and down stairs to see if her clothes were dry yet. Now it will be so much easier to do a load any time she needed, rather than waiting for dirty clothes to pile up to make her trips to the basement less frequent. The end result will be a slightly smaller downstairs bathroom; but with the additional bathroom upstairs, she didn't need a large space downstairs.

She had considered adding a Jacuzzi off the backyard deck, but decided that would have to wait for another time, maybe once Terri was through with college and on her own. The changes she was already making were more than she could afford on her social work salary. But interest rates were low and she had started a small private practice, which was supplementing her income a small amount now and had the potential to increase over time.

She had considered adding an office with a separate entrance to allow her to see clients at home but had decided against it. Better for now to keep her work life and private life separate, she thought. Besides, it didn't strike her as being cost-effective. Most of the changes she was making would increase the value of the home if she chose to move. Who knew what she would do once Terri was gone?

Kate got out of her car, house keys in hand as she led the way to her house. They sat down at the dining room table, which had been cleared previously for this purpose, and spread out the project drawings. She carefully looked over all of the expenses, trying to make sure nothing of importance was left out. Change orders were very costly, she had been told. It's best to try to avoid them whenever possible. However, the contractors didn't mind – more money for them.

"Would you like some coffee while I look over these," Kate offered. She was feeling a little uncomfortable with him just sitting there.

"That would be great." He followed Kate into the kitchen as she poured water into her coffee pot and waited for it to brew.

"It won't take too long," she said nervously to fill in the lull.

"No problem. Just think, in a few months you'll be sitting at that breakfast nook, drinking your coffee and reading the morning paper."

"That's the plan," she said, uncomfortably aware of his large frame in her small kitchen. Not that he was overweight. Quite the contrary. He was quite muscular. She could see ripples of muscle under his shirt. She was relieved once the coffee was done and they went back to the plans.

"I think you'll see that everything is as you requested. We made the adjustments you asked for. The material expenses are laid out clearly as well as labor. You realize, of course, that any changes after today may mean more cost."

"Yes, I'm aware of that." She was also aware of him, leaning close to her as they looked over everything together.

"Then do we have a deal?"

"How long do you think it will take?"

"It shouldn't take more than two months, assuming all the materials arrive without a glitch and the weather cooperates for the outdoor work."

"How soon can you start?"

"Once you sign that paper, I'll order the necessary material. I'm finishing up one job right now, but I should be able to get a crew over here sometime next week to get started."

"I'd appreciate it if you could finish before my daughter gets home in August."

"I'll do my best. Agreed?"

"Agreed." Kate took a deep breath, signed the final documents, and wrote out a check for the first installment on the total bill.

"Great, I look forward to working with you, Ms. Connors," he said, reaching out his hand.

"Kate, just Kate is fine," Kate said as she took his hand. She hadn't noticed before what beautiful eyes he had. Deep brown. "I hope you still feel that way when we are done," she added with a smile.

He smiled back in response. "Well then, just Kate, you can call me Tom. I'll be seeing you," he said as he let himself out.

What was she doing? She scolded herself. What was she thinking? Was she that desperate? He was cute. Why was she so preoccupied with men right now? First Frank and now this total stranger. Sure, she had just hired him to do a significant amount of work around her house, or actually his company. But what else did she know about him except that he was licensed, had a good reputation around the town and his bid had been reasonable. She probably won't see him for the rest of the summer. She didn't even know if he were married or not—was he?

Perhaps she had been too long without a man in her life. Perhaps it was just part of her empty nest syndrome, seeking to fill the emptiness with a meaningless affair, or a meaningful one, or, she didn't know what. Or maybe a fantasy. That's it. It was just a harmless fantasy. No reason to get upset over that. It'll pass with time. They always do.

She gulped down her coffee, grabbed a sandwich to eat on the run and hurried back to work, anxious to busy herself again in her work.

Except for checking her email for messages from Terri, Kate avoided her computer all week. Foolishness, she told herself as she pushed out of mind any thought of Frank. She stayed later each night and finally freed her desk of the backlog of paperwork. In fact, when Friday afternoon arrived and she actually was caught up, she felt at a loss. Certainly there must be something else for her to do.

"You've been busy this week," the shelter director said, dropping in on her. "This is the first time since you started that you've cleaned your desk. Miss her that bad?"

"What do you mean?"

"Miss Terri that bad? Don't think I don't notice what's going on here, not just with our girls, but with our staff as well. Didn't Terri leave last weekend?"

"Yes," Kate admitted.

"And you've been working late every night this week."

"Well, I had the time. I thought it was about time I got a few things taken care of."

"Look, it's not that I don't appreciate your work. I wish all our workers were as conscientious as you. But at this rate, you're going to be burned out before the summer is through. I don't need any burnt-out social workers. The world's already got enough of them."

The director's dark face didn't give away her age. Kate suspected she was in her mid-fifties. She had a Master in Counseling as well as a Master in Business Administration, both essential for successfully keeping a non-profit like the shelter operational. She could be very matronly, a second mother figure to the girls and staff one minute and as tough as nails when she needed to be. The girls appreciated her caring discipline. Staff appreciated her fairness, even when they disagreed.

"You've put in enough time this week. I know it's your weekend to be on call. Why don't you leave early, give yourself a break? Get away from here for a while."

Kate knew there was no sense arguing. And perhaps her boss was right. She was on call this weekend. That could mean spending the whole weekend here, or she may not be called at all. But why not get a break while she could?

Kate packed her briefcase, resisting the urge to add more work, stopped at the supermarket for a few groceries before heading home for the weekend.

The house seemed emptier than usual. Some stacks of lumber had been delivered during the day and left in her backyard. That was a hopeful sign. Maybe they actually will start on the addition and remodeling on Monday. Maybe they would be done in two months. She could always hope. She took Cookie for her walk in case she got paged later that evening and didn't have time to take her then. Cookie panted at her side, showing some effects of the warm weather, but happy to be moving freely. Both she and Cookie were drooping by the time they returned.

Tom Jensen was there, checking on the supplies that had been delivered and delivering more.

"Hi, I didn't expect to run into you," he said.

"Well, I'm on call all weekend so my boss sent me home early. Looks like you're ready to begin."

"Yup, first thing Monday morning you'll be hearing hammering and sawing."

"That's great. Thanks for warning me. I'll make sure I'm up and out of here."

"We will need to be able to get into your house during the day."

"That's all right. I'll leave the back door unlocked if I leave before your men arrive. If they leave before I get back they can lock it from the inside and pull it shut behind them."

"Sounds like a plan."

"Yeah," Kate stood awkwardly, not sure what else to say, aware of the drops of sweat streaming down her face. "Would you care for some lemonade?" she offered.

"Thanks for the offer but I better be getting home."

"Yeah, big plans for tonight?"

"No, just a quiet night at home."

"Oh," there, you idiot. He must be married, why else would he be spending a quiet night at home. She didn't see any wedding ring, but that didn't necessarily mean anything. Some men just didn't wear rings. "I guess I'll be seeing you then," she said as she prepared to enter her home.

"Looking forward to it," Tom said with a smile and a touch to his cap. "Maybe we can do it another day."

"What?"

"The lemonade. Maybe another day."

"Sure," Kate said as she walked through the door. Sure, fat chance. She must have looked like an idiot, she thought as she wiped herself down with a cold cloth. She threw open all of the downstairs windows and turned on the fan, hoping for a breeze. It really wasn't that hot. She was just hot from walking Cookie. That and the occasional hot-flash. Kate only used her air-conditioning on the hottest of days. Heat index one hundred degrees. She hated having the windows shut. It felt so confining.

All winter she looked forward to being able to open her windows and let fresh air in. No way was she going to be confined all summer as well. This was one advantage to Terri being gone. She didn't have to argue with her over the air conditioning. Terri had little of her inclination to be outside, preferring the world of electronics, computer games and MTV to the world of bugs and nature. She didn't understand being uncomfortable when the house could be kept at a perfect seventy degrees all year long via heating and air conditioning. Of course, she also didn't pay the bill for any of these conveniences.

Wait till she's on her own, Kate thought. Tears that were never far away where Terri was concerned came to her eyes. It will be different then. Terri gone, on her own. Not for a while yet. She still had high school and then college. Why rush things?

Kate took the paper to the back deck. She sat on the covered swing and read the paper while sipping iced tea. Now this was the life. She decided to have a sandwich on the porch for her dinner, as long as she was able to fend off any bugs. She reluctantly went inside around eight, fully expecting a call from the shelter any minute.

"Come on, girls. It's Friday night. We always have a crisis or two on Friday night. Maybe it's too early," she thought.

Unsure what to do, she decided to check her email once again, then decided to play around on the Internet. What harm could it do?

She returned again to the Website that mentioned Frank's dad and date of death: October 13, 1985. It didn't list a cause. Was it in the line of duty, she wondered? Probably not. They usually mention stuff like that. She went back to the picture of Frank. Under significant achievements he had a number of medals. He must have been good at what he did. She wondered again why he left, what he had done. No reason was given and there were no additional entries available.

It must have had something to do with his dad's death. That must have been why he left active duty. She imagined him, let's see, 1985, age 29, so young! Much too young to have done all that he had done. Much too young to lose his dad. His dad must have been young, too, when he died. Only fifty-two. She imagined Frank going into a deep depression, quitting the service in protest, in anger. Maybe he had a wife and a child, a baby boy, three or four, hardly old enough to remember his granddad. His young wife didn't know how to cope with her husband's change, wasn't sure what to do.

But Frank pulled out of it. Of course, he did. He got his life back together, to his wife's relief, although he never completely got over his dad's death. You don't get over these things, you just get on. So that's what he did, becoming a commercial airline pilot. The pay was good, but once again there were all those nights gone, leaving his wife and their son.

Kate imagined her, pretty, blonde hair, sparkling smile, but anyone can get lonely left home alone too much. And then, of course, Frank never opened up to his wife when he was home—typical male! Or maybe he tried but she didn't understand, or couldn't handle it, afraid of what he was trying to tell her. Some things are just better left unsaid, or at least not said to family. Kate knew that. And so they drifted apart and eventually divorced.

That's how Kate imagined it. Wonder if he ever thought of me, she thought. Not that she had thought about him during that time.

She had been married too, young mother, working part-time while trying to be a full-time wife and mother. Their days in the peace movement over, she and Dick had eventually married and settled into a fairly comfortable routine. Both were in service professions at first. Slowly they had moved further and further from their ideals till now they were unrecognizable amidst their middle class lifestyle and values.

Dick had gone to law school, first with an eye to helping the most disadvantaged, offering pro-bono assistance at legal services; but as they faced mounting bills from his education and she decided to further her own education, he had gone into corporate law, thereby saving them financially but losing each other in the process. They just grew apart. It's hard to say when and how it happened, but it did. These things do.

There were some discrepancies on the website. It said Frank left active service in 1985 but it also said he served in Desert Storm. Wasn't that several years later? Maybe he had continued on as a reservist, helping out when called. Maybe he had been called to serve in Afghanistan and Iraq. So many questions and no answers. She wasn't sure how to get more information. You'd think they would update the information on the site. But no, they didn't. Reluctantly she shut off the computer and went to bed.

The weekend dragged on forever. She had not made any plans because of being on-call. It was so hard to have to change plans at the last minute due to an emergency. Rather than deal with the hassle, she had made no plans. And, of course, since she had no plans that could be disrupted, there had been no calls, except for a minor situation one of the weekend staff had a question about, a situation easily handled by phone. Kate had to fight the urge to drop by the shelter. What would her boss have said then?

She might as well emblazon it on her forehead: LOSER. I have no life outside my daughter and my work. And by now all her friends had plans for the weekend. It was too short notice to do anything with them. They all had families and lives that kept them busy.

Terri was right. She needed to get a life. She didn't think the weekend would ever end, but then it was Monday morning and, sure enough, a work crew showed up in her backyard about the time she had to leave – a work crew of two. Kate had envisioned a work crew of eight descending on her house en masse and finishing the job in one week. After all, if Habitat for Humanity can build a whole house in a week, certainly they could do this job in one week. They set about sawing, measuring and hammering so that by the time Kate came home the frame for the addition was already up.

This would be the easy work, all on the outside of the house. They wouldn't start tearing out walls until this was completed. Fortunately, Kate had enough room on the side of her house to provide the necessary space without removing the deck. The breakfast nook would expand part way onto the deck but not enough to take away from the overall area. Unfortunately the mess left by the construction took away from the appeal of the deck. No longer did she look out on a yard secluded from the neighbors by a row of trees and bushes, but at a pile of wood and other construction material. She just hoped the grass wasn't ruined during the process.

The week sped by, between work and watching the progress on her house. She found that the largest work crew she saw all week was three, but at least they were making good progress. She thought they might even have the exterior work done by the weekend.

This weekend she was going to be prepared. No more sitting home all alone all weekend. She wasn't on call, so she decided to take advantage of the time to pack Cookie in the car and visit her parents. It had become harder and harder to find time to visit as Terri got older and more reluctant to leave her friends and computer for a boring weekend at Grandma and Grandpa's.

Her parents had refused to enter the computer world. Terri couldn't imagine staying even one day anywhere without Internet access. It just wasn't done. It was a relief not having to work around Terri's schedule. It was a relief not having to listen to her complaining as she dragged her kicking and screaming to Kate's hometown. It was nice to visit, although after a weekend she was definitely ready to go home.

The first day was always nice. It was nice to have someone else cooking meals and looking out for you. But by Sunday it felt to Kate like she had regressed to being a child again. When her mom started in on her love life, or lack of one, Kate knew it was time to go.

"Oh, Mom."

"Well, you're not getting any younger, you know." As if Kate needed to be reminded of that fact. There were enough daily reminders each time she looked in the mirror. "I would just feel better knowing there was someone to take care of you."

"And I can't take care of myself?"

"No, you know what I mean." Kate did know what she meant. In her mom's eyes she needed a man to lean on, to protect her and help her, not a bad idea. There were days when Kate thought the same thing. It would be nice to have someone else to help with all of the daily chores and problems of life, but she was doing just fine on her own. And even when she had that "someone" in her life, it didn't necessarily make things easier. Actually, it just was more complicated. She didn't need complications.

She casually picked up the phone book, randomly looking at names, wondering if any of her friends from high school had moved back to the area. She saw some of their parents' names still listed but not theirs. Must be they had been like her. Once out of Morenci there really wasn't any compelling reason to return. She saw Shaughnessy listed in the book. That must be Frank's grandparents, she thought. They couldn't possibly still be around. They had been old when she had known them.

"Dad ...," she walked from where she had been standing in the kitchen to the living room. Her dad was sitting in his rocker recliner reading the paper. He would know if anyone knew. He usually kept track of people's comings and goings. As a pharmacist and owner of the local pharmacy, he had gotten to know most of the residents of Morenci until he retired after the arrival of the new Walgreen's in the strip mall outside of town. He had been close to retirement anyway, so he gracefully sold out his business before being forced out.

"Yeah," he grumbled from behind his paper.

"I see the Shaughnessy's are still listed at their old address in the phone book. Are they still around?"

"She is. He died about six years ago. Stroke, it was. She probably didn't want to change the name. She doesn't get out much."

"Do you hear anything about their grandson, Frank?"

"The one you dated in high school?"

"Yes."

"He died," her dad said. "I don't remember when, a while ago, before his grandfather died."

"You mean his dad had died."

"No, the son too. All the Shaughnessy men. Some kind of heart trouble. They both had it. His grandmother is still around. We used to see her now and then, but not anymore. She doesn't get out too much."

Kate had felt her heart leap into her throat once again, just like when she had read the original obituary for Frank's dad. It couldn't be true.

"Really?" she had asked, trying to mask any emotion.

"Those Shaughnessy men are all short-lived. Runs in the family," her mom said, joining them from the kitchen.

"When did it happen?" she asked again.

"Oh, I don't remember. A while ago," her dad stated then went back to his paper. She had wanted to insist he was mistaken, but she knew that wouldn't change anything. Still she found it very hard to believe.

How sad for Frank's grandmother, Kate had thought, losing her husband, son and grandson. How many losses can one heart take? Kate wondered about sending her a card of condolences. Would it just stir up more hurt, or would it be helpful? Would Frank's grandmother even remember who she was? Kate decided she would send one for her own sake, to help put some closure on this part of her life.

It still didn't seem possible he was gone. Part of her continued in denial. If only she could have found an obituary somewhere. Then it would have been more real to her, but she hadn't found anything on the Internet.

She wondered, how had it happened? When? And why was it so important to her? Why was she obsessing over his death? She finally decided she needed to just let it be. Sometimes time does run out.

And now, here she was, a whole summer stretching out before her and nowhere to go, no-one to spend it with.

She had been anxious to get back to her computer and see if she had any messages from Terri. Terri was right. It was hard to go for a day without a computer. It was like going back in time. She checked her email, sent off a quick message to Terri, then found herself once again drawn to Frank's picture. The same face stared back at her. There was still no new information. You'd think they'd at least post an obituary, but no.

"Hey, Chad."

"Yeah," the soldier responded.

"Aren't we supposed to be looking for any unusual activity on our website?"

"Yeah. You got something?" The young soldier walked from his computer monitor and peered over the other soldier's shoulders.

"There seems to be some unusual activity on the sites with information about your dad and granddad. Take a look. Looks like somebody is trying to get information on your family."

"It's probably nothing. Let's see, katydid56 @ yahoo.com. Looks like it's coming from somewhere in Ohio. My great grandmother still lives around there. Maybe it's someone who knew my granddad. Let's see, email address belongs to a Kathleen Connors."

"Don't you think you should alert your dad? With all the high security information he's been handling, he should know if someone is trying to get information about him."

"Won't hurt to let him know. I'll email him the name, see if he recognizes it." Chad returned to his own computer, sent the message, then stepped back.

"You hungry?" he asked. "I'm going to get something to eat. You want me to bring you back anything?"

"No, I'm fine. Oh, and Chad," he turned away from his monitor to grin at him, "Say hi to Cindy for me."

Chad smiled and walked away.

Kate had been pleased with the progress on her house that first week but was dismayed when no-one showed up Monday morning when she left for work. "Maybe they're running late," she had thought. When she came home at lunchtime to check on their progress and still no one was there, she picked up her phone.

"Is Mr. Jensen in?" she asked the receptionist.

"One moment, please. Who shall I say is calling?"

"Kate Connors."

"Hi Kate, how can I help you?" Kate jumped as she heard Tom's deep voice over the phone.

"Oh, it's you. I half expected to be put on hold and then told you were unavailable."

"No, I was eating my lunch in my office today. What's up?"

"There's no one here."

"Yeah. Because of the long weekend for the fourth coming up, some of the guys wanted to take the whole week off. They'll be back next week."

"But what about finishing by mid-August?"

"They'll just have to work extra hard, won't they?"

"I guess so."

"Anything else I can help you with?"

"No, I guess not."

"You have a great Fourth of July."

"Yeah, right." The conversation left Kate far from satisfied. But what did she know about construction. Maybe they'll still be done before Terri gets home. At least he hadn't brushed her off or ignored her call. She guessed she would have to trust him. Why had she hired his company for the job if she couldn't trust him? She trusted him about as much as anybody in construction after all the horror stories she had heard. Nothing she could do about it right now, anyway.

Happy Fourth! Big deal. It would be no holiday for her. She had agreed to work at the shelter to let other employees have the holiday with their families. She didn't have any family around. The girls at the shelter were as close as she came to family right now. They could have some fun though. Maybe a picnic in the park, then watch the fireworks from the roof of the shelter. They were in a pretty close proximity to the fireworks. Not as good as the park, but at least they could see without having to fight crowds or having to haul the babies with them and keep them up beyond their bedtime. It actually might be fun.

And it was. The long weekend passed surprisingly quickly. Kate was happy to hear the sound of hammering once again as she left for work Monday morning. Only three – but at least they were on the job again. Over the course of the week, at times there was only one worker, sometimes two, sometimes three, but at least there was progress. They had sealed off the outside portion of the addition and knocked a hole through her wall to work on the inside, wiring, plumbing, dry wall, etc. Kate was only too glad to leave the house each day. Soon they would be knocking down more walls and begin the really messy phase of the project.

She noted the progress each day and tried to quiz the workers when she had the chance. Better that she wasn't around, she told herself. She'd drive herself and everyone else crazy.

"Hmm," Frank paused and wondered at his latest email from Chad. "Do I know anyone named Kathleen Connors? No why should I?" he had responded. Kathleen from Ohio, katydid56 @ yahoo.com. He had known a Katy one time, had dated her the summer before his senior year in high school. But her last name had been Jackson and she had lived in Michigan. Of course Connors could be her married name and who's to say she couldn't move to Ohio. Certainly wasn't a whole lot to keep her in Morenci, that was sure.

There hadn't been anything to keep him in Morenci, except her. He had wanted to stay with his grandparents and finish high school in Morenci because of her. It had been a crazy idea even for his teen self. He would have gone crazy stuck in that little town with one Movie Theater and one pizza parlor to its name. He had been better off at the base with his family, even if he did have to, once again, attend a new high school. There was more to do. And then there were the planes. How he had loved watching them, hanging out around them, learning what he could. He loved flying. Yes, Morenci had been no place for him.

Still, he wondered. What would have happened if he had stayed with his grandparents that year? A year in a real town – not a military base. How would his life have changed, or would it have

30

changed? Perhaps if he had had a more "normal" childhood instead of moving from one base to another, he would have been different, his life would have been different. Chances are he never would have gone into the military. Not that he regretted it, not that it wasn't a good life.

It was the only life he had known growing up. No wonder he had stayed in the life as an adult. Maybe if he had had that year away from the base he would have chosen a different path, or maybe he would have chosen the same path – only it would have been a choice based on real options, not just doing what was expected of him.

What's done is done. Nothing can be changed now. Still, sometimes he wondered. He had wanted something different for his son. Wanted him to be settled, have a home he could call his own, friends he could grow up with, a neighborhood. He had wanted him to grow up in a regular community, not a military community. When his father died he just couldn't do it anymore. He knew it was time to get out. He had worked first as a commercial pilot, then when the long trips away from home got to be too much, he joined the ground crew as a mechanic. He made good pay, better than in the service.

He had only been twenty-nine when his dad had died. Chad had only been five. He hadn't started school yet. It was time to settle out and settle down. His wife had been happy at first. She had never quite accepted life on a military base as an officer's wife. There were responsibilities that came with the position.

He remembered her reaction when he had first mentioned the possibility of leaving the military.

"Oh, Frank, that would be wonderful. We can have a real home and Chad could go to the same school while growing up instead of moving from one base to another." She had hugged him. "And maybe I could get a job, once we are settled and Chad is in school."

"Whoa, I just said I was thinking about it."

"Well think harder and faster," she said pulling away from him. "Yesterday is not too soon for me. No more long stints worrying about whether you will return. I've tried, Frank, I have, but it's been hard."

"I know, baby. I'm sorry I didn't recognize it sooner."

"That's in the past. Let's put it behind us and focus on our future."

She had been delighted at the prospect of a permanent home, getting Chad settled into a school and going back to work herself. The long hours away as a pilot had been hard on her, yet not as bad as the stints overseas in the military. When he finally had more regular hours as a mechanic he had not received the same enthusiastic reaction.

"No more flights overseas, being gone days at a time. I'll have a regular schedule, be able to help more with Chad, attend his after school activities."

"That's nice, honey," she had said, hardly looking up from the book she was reading. She had gotten so accustomed to him being gone that she couldn't handle having him around. So eventually they divorced. It seemed the only thing keeping them together had been the fact they had so little time together, that and Chad. Chad had been fifteen when they finally split.

Frank had gotten an apartment close to the airport and not too far from Chad. He had wanted so much for Chad to have what he hadn't – a stable home, the chance to grow up in one house, one neighborhood with life-long friends. There was no way he was going to take that away from him. He didn't need a house.

Sandy got the home with no argument from him. Chad now had two homes, one with his mother, one with him. He had known the house Frank had not had growing up but not the home, Frank thought with some pain. At least his parents' marriage had made it, withstood the struggles of military life. His hadn't been able to withstand civilian life, Frank thought.

Frank had not left the military service entirely. When at war with Iraq, his services as a pilot were required. He had helped with Operation Desert Storm. And Chad, even though technically not a military brat, was a military brat. He had had a choice, many choices. He chose to follow in his father's and grandfather's footsteps.

After September 11, 2001, Frank's plans shifted again. He was no longer married. His son no longer lived at home. He had lost some good friends in the attack. It was time to go back into service for his country, he told himself. What did he have to lose?

Kate Jackson. He paused and looked back at the email Chad had sent him. *Haven't thought about her in years. Could Kathleen Connors be Kate Jackson?* He sent another email to his son.

"Could you check her maiden name and see if she ever lived in Morenci, Michigan?"

III

Okay, so now it was official. She was the new town crank. How was she to know that everyone else within a mile radius of the offending noise was deaf or had air conditioning and so slept blissfully through the night, not awakened by "She's my Lady" at 3 a.m. and "Born in the USA" at 5 a.m. and God only knows what that sound was at quarter to seven. She looked over at her sleeping husband. How could he snore away through all of this? She was tempted to whack him on the side of his head, but what good would that have done? Then they both would have been awake and tired during the day.

By quarter to eight she could take it no longer. She crawled out of bed and called the village office to register her complaint, fulfilling her civic duty, confident that hers would be but one of many; that others living even closer to the offending noise and able to identify street and house number would complain as well. Certainly she couldn't call the police for such a minor infraction, besides which, the culprits were too smart. They cranked the music up on two or three songs every hour or two and then lowered it back to an inaudible level. This lulled you into thinking the worst was over, until you were hit by another blast. And, of course, if you were to call the police, by the time they arrived the offenders would be quietly tending their grill, blending into the scenery with other holiday revelers.

Now she was as patriotic as the next person. She'd have been happy to celebrate the Fourth of July by singing "Born in the USA" at the top of her lungs with or without accompaniment at a decent hour, say seven o'clock or eight, or maybe as late as nine, had even done so on occasion, but certainly not at 5 a.m. That was when she was routinely awakened by songbirds each morning, after which she flipped back on her other side and went back to sleep for another hour or two.

Sure, it had been the Fourth of July, but some, like her, had to work on the fifth. And so she called and left her complaint on the answering machine at the village office at quarter to eight, then left for work five minutes later. She picked up the remnants of some fireworks that must have been launched from her back yard.

As she drove through the neighborhood she tried to pinpoint the location of the noise and perhaps have a word or two with the culprits, but all was deceptively quiet. When she called an hour later from her office to check on the status of her complaint, she found that hers was the sole complaint. Thus she became the village crank. She was sure that heads turned as she walked to the post office and library and people commented on the crazy lady living alone with two cats who heard noises during the night and didn't know enough to keep them to herself. She was the old fogey in a neighborhood of old fogies, most of whom were ten to twenty years her senior. The fact that she didn't live alone didn't make a difference.

She wasn't sure how it happened or when it happened. It just did. These things happen in small towns. Like the mythical Lake Wobegone of Prairie Home Companion, a small town has a life of its own, not defined by the residents who live there but by the town itself. Someone had to fill the role of the crazy cat lady and town crank who called every week with a complaint about something, so why not she? Could she help it that her recycling or garbage was often overlooked, forcing her to call to have them picked up? Or that because of the quiet street she lived on, only one block long, she was now and then forgotten by the paper carrier, forcing her to call and request a paper. Certainly none of these were her doing. And so she was victim of the town's need to have someone to label in this position.

At over fifty she figured she fit the bill. She felt every bit of her fifty years. If seventy was the new fifty, she figured that made her thirty. So why did she feel like seventy, as her bones crackled more than her cereal? Snap, crackle, pop. And of course, the sounds that emanated from other orifices on her body. She was a veritable one-woman band. She was still waiting for that post-menopausal burst of energy she had heard about in her forties. She was past menopause with still no new-found confidence that comes from no longer being enslaved to the rages of estrogen and "cycles."

Her children, grown and living on their own, had yet to produce any grandchildren. You would think that was the least they could do after all she had sacrificed for them. It was about time they settled down and got busy producing grandchildren, maybe two or three at a time to make up for making her wait so long.

She was restless. She wanted do something, something "great," something "outstanding," with what time she had left. She wanted to go out in a blaze of glory, cats and all. But instead, she was stuck in this town, in this house, like a character in that Jimmy Stewart movie, "It's a Wonderful Life," only it didn't feel so wonderful. No wonder she was the town crank! Her degrees meant nothing.

"How was your Fourth?" she called her sister.

"Uneventful."

"Mine, too, until three o'clock in the morning when a neighbor blasted his music at a decibel designed to break the sound barrier. Don slept through it. Men!"

"You have a busy day today? Maybe we could get together?"

"I've got a full day of classes, maybe tomorrow."

Her disrupted sleep came back to haunt her that day as this was her heavy day, only two classes to teach Monday and Thursday, but they were longer than during the rest of the school year because the summer term was shorter. Tuesday and Wednesday were free for the interminable faculty meetings, although these were fewer during the summer, and then the inevitable paperwork. Friday she had to herself.

She slogged through her classes, happy that they were old standbys, classes she had been teaching off and on for the past fifteen years. She could have done them in her sleep, which wasn't far from reality that day as she silently cursed the noisemaker. Maybe it was time to move. She had considered this so many times over the years, especially since her youngest had left for college in New York. New York, the Big Apple. She had been sure she would never see her again. She had lost her to the big city, Helen had thought, yet Lindsey had been the one who had returned, setting up an art studio in the "city" a short drive from her home.

She loved the quiet of small town life. Aside from the occasional loud parties or listening to her neighbors bicker on

Sunday morning, it was a good life. Still she was restless. Thirteen years of teaching philosophy and ethics to young minds, but what had she accomplished? Perhaps the world was a better place, but perhaps not.

The new millennium had been born without the new consciousness she had hoped for, believed in during the sixties. The hundredth monkey, the non-violent revolution. Somehow as you changed hearts and minds one person at a time, they were going to eventually reach a critical mass and then – then a new world order would erupt. Then we would finally be a global community, no longer holding countries at bay with nuclear weapons. We would learn to live together, or would die together in global destruction.

She had yet to see that global community or massive conversion, although it did seem that we were connected more than we realized through multi-national corporations, that maybe countries, as we know them, would someday be a creation of the past.

She had posed that question to her class, "What if someday, countries as we know them no longer existed? What if multi-nationals became the ruling powers?"

"They already are," one of her students responded.

"And what would that look like?" she asked.

"Not too good. Greed would be the ruling principle," he responded.

"Not necessarily, being good business people, they would recognize the need to not destroy the world and that they needed a workforce. They would have an incentive to keep us from destroying ourselves with nuclear weapons, or even bit by bit through global warming and pollution."

"That hasn't kept them from doing this so far. They are faceless entities, welding enormous amounts of power with no accountability. At least our elected officials are held accountable. We know who they are and can vote against them."

"Yeah, that's what is scary about these multinationals."

The debate continued. Those were the good days, when students were interested and engaged.

After thirteen years she felt that she had barely made a difference. Ethics was more essential than ever, being so lacking in the world. It seemed like it was getting worse despite her best efforts to impart the knowledge of great thinkers to young minds, despite her efforts to impress on them ethical standards. She wanted one last hurrah before she died, to make an impact or die trying.

That had been last year, the Fourth of July. That had been before 9/11. Had she actually forgotten her husband, or maybe they had forgotten each other along the way? Either way, she guessed that disqualified her for the position of cat lady, leaving only the crank job. She figured she was qualified for that.

She had pursued the mommy track, giving up teaching once her first baby had been born, but not giving up education entirely. She had continued her education, slowly racking up credits for her Master's Degree and then a PhD in Philosophy. Why? She didn't know. It had interested her at the time. It wasn't exactly a money maker. Many philosophy majors worked in fast food restaurants or other minimum wage jobs along with English majors. She hadn't needed the money. Don made a good income by then, having moved up the ranks to a management position in the local power company. Everybody needed gas and electric. He had a solid, stable job with an income they could count on. So she had taken courses that interested her.

Once her daughters started school, she commenced teaching as a sub, thereby keeping her teaching skills honed. She also had become involved in the local community, first by serving on the PTA and then the school board. When she had learned through one of her contacts about a position opening at a local college for teaching Philosophy and Ethics, she had put in her application on a whim and been surprised when called for an interview.

"Dr. Peterson?"

"Yes."

"This is Ron Carpenter, the Dean of the Philosophy Department at Arbor University. You interviewed with us for a position."

"Yes, I did."

"We are interested in offering you the position. When can you come in so we can work out details?"

She had put the phone down in a daze.

"What's up, Mom?" Allyson asked her.

"I've been offered the job teaching Philosophy."

"That's great," Allyson said.

"Yeah, Mom, go for it," Lindsey chimed in.

And so it had been settled. By then her daughters had been starting high school and middle school. They had less need for her to supervise the practical necessities of daily life and more need for freedom. They had thought it a good idea. The hours were good with summer vacation, unless you chose to teach summer classes as she had this year, spring break and Christmas vacation, so she had said yes. That had been thirteen years ago. Since that time her daughters, now twenty-seven and twenty-five respectively had finished high school and college and left home for careers of their own. Her husband was anticipating an early retirement at fifty-eight after over thirty years on the job. He was anxious to be free of his nine-to-five schedule.

She wasn't sure what she wanted. It seemed her life had gone from bad to worse since the summer. The freshmen in her Introduction to Philosophy courses just kept getting younger every year. It couldn't be that she was getting older. They weren't interested in philosophy, had no aptitude for the science, but were only taking it to fulfill a humanities requirement.

One young man leaned back in his seat with his head hanging, eyes half closed. Others slouched forward, heads nodding. I dare you to teach me anything, their body language screamed. In the back of class one young man was giggling, his laptop in front of him supposedly for taking notes. He nudged the woman next to him. Helen walked to the back of the room, talking the whole time, till she reached him. She looked at the laptop to see a YouTube video of a cat. Was this middle school or what? Do I have to confiscate his computer, she wondered? Hadn't she left this behind when she had quit her job teaching middle school in order to raise her daughters?

Yet here they were, back in her classroom with the same attitudes. Perhaps scariest of all was the young woman who sat bolt upright in the front row, her eyes wide open as if held by tooth picks. What was she on? And to think someone was paying good money for the privilege of them sitting here.

Helen hadn't changed, so it must be them. Sure she revised her syllabus and lesson plans every year to accommodate the demands of different classes, but the essentials remained the same. She didn't see a need to completely revamp her course. The early Greeks, Plato, Aristotle, hadn't written anything new last that she had heard. They were still foundational, as were Hegel and Sartre. So why was she meeting so much more resistance this year as opposed to previous years? Perhaps this generation just wasn't interested. Or perhaps it was just one of those years, one of those classes that doesn't mesh well. All teachers have those at times. She had been teaching long enough to have experienced this before.

It's amazing how different each class is, just as different as each individual is. These different individuals come together to make a unique class with its own dynamics. There are those years when everything comes together; students are actually somewhat interested and receptive to what you have to teach them. Even those years have challenges, but those are the good years when you feel you are making a difference in a young person's life, when you feel you are making a positive contribution. It's that which keeps you going as a teacher, not the money.

And then there are those classes like the ones she had had that fall when it seemed nothing she did could reach these students. As the Chinese proverb says, "When the student is ready, the teacher comes." What do you do when you are being paid to teach but the students aren't ready? The events of September 11 hadn't helped. It had just served to make her feel even more irrelevant. Certainly there was something better she could be doing with her time.

A hand went up in back as she went over the syllabus. "What does Plato have to do with what's going on today? Why are we studying people who lived thousands of years ago when there are people dying here and now in our own country, when our country is under attack?"

"Why indeed? Let's talk about it. Are the Greeks still relevant to life today? They were warriors." She had tried to engage their interest, but no luck.

Maybe it was just she who was irrelevant. Or maybe God was trying to tell her something, that it was time to try something different.

She rushed through her emails. There were the usual ones, the weekly newsletter which reiterated what had been said in last week's newsletter. She scanned for new items then sent it to the trash. There were notices from campus safety about parking and reminders about upcoming meetings.

"Wait …" Helen's finger paused over the delete, "something about a sabbatical." There it was: the yearly reminder about applying for a sabbatical. She clicked and opened the file, read through the requirements and thought, "I can do this."

Maybe she just needed some time off for rest and renewal. Maybe that was the problem. Or maybe it was time for a change? Maybe that was God's not-so-subtle way of telling her about the other plans God had for her life. Don had been pleased at her plans for a sabbatical year.

"That's great. I can retire at the same time and we can finally do all those things we haven't had time to do. Spend the summer in Europe, maybe take a cruise. I'll check into it."

"Wait, I haven't even applied for the sabbatical yet, much less get it."

"Don't worry, you will, and when you do we will be prepared. You can't plan these things overnight." That hadn't been her vision. She had talked it over with Kate at lunch the next day.

"I'm thinking about applying for a sabbatical."

"That would be great. What would you do during that time?"

"That's the problem. You usually are supposed to use the time to pursue some educational goal. I've already got a doctorate. I'm not interested in post-doctoral work. I guess I could say I was working on a book. That's always a good one. Don wants us to travel, see Europe."

"Oh, I've got it. Go to Greece, to all those places where the dead people you teach about used to live."

"I don't know."

"What's not to know? Touring the Greek isles, maybe meeting a handsome Greek fisherman . . ." Kate sighed as she stared off into space, caught up in her own fantasy.

"This trip is supposed to be about me, not you."

"At least let me live vicariously through you."

"And what about Don?"

"We can arrange to have him shipwrecked on a remote island. You can be the frantic wife whose husband is rescued by a dashing Greek, someone like Fabio."

"And what happens to this Fabio character once Don is back?"

"That's where I come in."

"Thanks, but no thanks. You are going to have to find your Fabio on your own. Why don't you go to Greece?"

"Without you? What would be the fun in that? Besides, there's Terri to consider – and who's got money to travel? I'm just finishing paying off my student loans. I have to start saving for Terri's college expenses."

"What about her dad? He's got money. How'd the move to California go? Maybe Terri could stay with him while you cruise."

"Bite your tongue. That's the problem. He wants her to come for the summer. How can I live without her all summer?"

"What does Terri want to do?'

"She hasn't decided yet."

"No sense in inviting trouble. Wait till she decides. Then you can obsess."

"I guess . . . so back to you and that Greek vacation. Maybe you can take me?" Lunch with Kate had been fun, but she still didn't know what she wanted to do. For some reason she had felt little enthusiasm for her husband's travel plans. She wasn't ready to retire from the work force yet. She just wanted a break. There was still work for her to do, she just wasn't sure what. She wanted to make a difference. Yes, she had been forming young minds for thirteen years. Yes, the world definitely needed young adults who understood ethics and principles for ethical decision-making, but was that enough?

Maybe it was time for her to leave the world of academia for the "real world," whatever that was. Maybe it was time for her to put into practice what she had been teaching for so many years. She had former students who were in the business world, business men and women, hopefully using ethics in their dealings. She had former students who were lawyers, teachers, politicians, some who had gone into the medical field. But what could she do besides teach?

She had yet to file the paperwork for the sabbatical. She had until the end of January. She had to come up with something soon. She had been glad for the interruption when the phone rang.

"May I speak with Helen Peterson?"

"Speaking."

"Helen, you may not remember me. We met at Republican headquarters. Cheryl Anderson. I worked for Representative Chalmers' campaign. I was wondering if we could talk some time."

"What about?"

"We were wondering if you might be interested in running for local state representative. Can we set up a time to talk?"

"What? Where did this come from? Are you sure you have the right Helen Peterson?"

"We were impressed with your volunteer work, not just for the Republican Party but in the community. We think you have potential."

"Oh, okay, I guess. Let me get my calendar," Helen said as she fumbled for her purse and dug out her calendar and a pen.

Helen arranged to meet Cheryl over lunch the next week. She had continued to be active in her community over the years, continuing to serve on committees even after her stint on the school board was over. She had served on the school board and the board for a number of non-profit organizations, and had volunteered for the Republican Party. Yet she had never considered running for office herself.

"We are aware of all of your community service, the boards you have served on. We don't currently have a strong candidate for the upcoming election. Your name was mentioned as a possibility. What do you think?"

"I don't have any political experience."

"We'll take care of that. You have experience public speaking from your teaching, are known in the community, and you teach ethics. What better combination for a politician?"

Helen didn't quite see it that way, but she found herself saying yes. She had her sabbatical plan. She could explore the ethics of local politics. It had not been something she had been considering, but here it was, the right offer at the right time. A chance to do some good for the community. Maybe this had been what God had in store for her.

Don didn't think so.

"But what about spending the summer in Europe, staying in bed and breakfasts, enjoying the countryside, the museums, the culture? What about that?"

"That was your dream, Don, not mine. You hardly know me."

"All the more reason to take this trip, to get reacquainted after all these years of raising children and working, living two separate lives. We need this. Our marriage needs this."

"But maybe I don't need it, not now anyway. Maybe I need to at least give this a try. I may not make it past the primary. We can always go on our trip after that."

"And if you are elected?"

"I guess we will deal with it then."

Reluctantly Don had agreed to put off making any plans until after the primary.

Her winter courses had gone surprising well after the difficult fall. Of course she only had the one freshman course, her other classes consisted of upperclassmen who were either majoring or minoring in philosophy or taking the course because of interest. It almost made her question whether she had been too quick to request a sabbatical, but still a year off from teaching wasn't forever. She could come back ready for new challenges and if she chose not to come back, at least she would be ending on a better note than the previous semester.

Helen finished up her classes and submitted her grades in May. Then she began full-fledged campaigning, going to community events, fund-raisers, parades, door-to-door, town meetings, pressing the flesh. She wasn't entirely sure what she was doing, but she found herself being carried along by the momentum, becoming more and more excited as she fleshed out her stand on issues, what she would do if elected and studied everything she could on the ins and outs of state politics. She studied policies and laws enacted over the past fifty years, learned who the key players were, the movers and shakers in her party and recruited their help.

This year the Fourth of July found her campaigning, walking in the parade, shaking hands and kissing babies at local picnics. When her neighbor woke her up once again with loud music, she rolled over in bed, dead to the world, then slept late.

But, I being poor, have only my dreams;
I have spread my dreams under your feet;
tread softly because you tread on my dreams.
William Butler Yeats

IV

Five weeks into Terri's summer trip, four weeks into construction, if you could count July Fourth week. Three weeks till Terri got home. There was no way this remodeling would be done by then. Kate had Tom's phone number on speed dial. Kate and his receptionist, Pam, were on a first-name basis. Pam knew it was Kate the minute she picked up the phone and heard Kate's voice. Progress was going so slow. There were days when Kate was sure the workers must have left her house as soon as she left for work. She'd come home expecting to see something, any sign of progress.

"I'm sorry. I had to pull the guys off of your home for another job we are working on. Just couldn't spare anyone. But don't worry. It'll get done. Once we get this other job finished, you'll have a full work crew."

"And that would entail two men?"

"Hey, I may even be able to throw in a third one." And then when they were there, she'd come home and find the work hadn't been done the way she wanted it. At first she had tried to give them the benefit of the doubt. Better not to interfere. Then when she did try to talk to them she was given the run-around and told she had to take it up with the boss. That was why she ended up talking to Tom so often and that was why he ended up at her house that Friday at four thirty in the afternoon.

"What seems to be the problem?"

"Wasn't the window supposed to be here? And the flooring. That wasn't what I had picked. And the faucets are all wrong." Kate began her laundry list.

"No, this is right. You're reading the blueprint wrong. That wasn't exactly what you had wanted but I got a really good deal on that particular linoleum. It's a better quality than what we had originally planned and the pattern's a fairly close match, but we can get the other if you want." One by one he went over every spot of the building, answering her questions till she couldn't think of any more. She started to feel foolish about all of her complaints.

"I'm sorry for taking up so much of your time. I really appreciate it."

"Just doing my job."

"Well, I don't know too many men who would be so patient with all my questions. I'm sorry I kept you so late." Kate looked at the clock. Five thirty. "You'll be late getting home."

"No problem. Why don't we get something to eat?"

"Oh, I don't know. What about your family?"

"Don't have any, at least not at home. No-one's waiting for me. We both need to eat. Why not eat together. That way if you have any more questions you can ask them over dinner."

"Right now?"

"I would like to change. How about I pick you up at seven?"

"Okay, I'll see you then." Did she just agree to a date? No, more like a business dinner, or a dinner between friends, not a date, she told herself as she watched him drive away. What shall I wear, she thought in a panic. Where were they going? Something casual, maybe. Nothing fancy. He didn't strike her as the fancy type, but then what did she know about him. She opted for dress slacks, sandals and a summer top. Casual, and yet dressy.

She was relieved when he arrived in khakis and a polo shirt. She had guessed right.

"Ready to go?" he asked when she answered the door.

"Sure," Kate responded as she grabbed her purse.

They ate outside at a small bistro downtown, enjoying the clear summer night. They munched on deli sandwiches washed down with beer and watched people walk by on the walkway that framed either side of the river. Kate kept noticing the ripple of muscle under his shirt, how his teeth shined under his mustache and how he kept brushing back his bushy brown hair. And, of course, there were those eyes.

Outside of her home, Kate found herself tongue-tied. She didn't know what to say.

"Tell me about yourself," Tom requested.

"Not much to tell. I'm a single parent."

"Yes, the elusive Terri. The invisible teen who's pending arrival strikes fear into all of my workers' hearts. Not because of what she might do, but because of what her mother might do if we aren't done by then. I'm beginning to wonder if you just made her up to have a reason to taunt and push my workers to meet your deadline."

"She's no imaginary child. See, here's her picture." Kate handed him a picture from her purse.

"Why, she looks quite ordinary, not at all someone to put fear into hearts."

"Let me assure you, she's far from ordinary. And not just because I'm her mother."

"An extraordinary woman like you would have to have an extraordinary child."

"I didn't say that. What about you? Any children?"

"Three boys. All grown up and gone, although the youngest has been working with me this summer, while home from college." Tom showed her their pictures.

"And their mother?" Kate asked.

"Here she is with the boys when they were small. She died ten years ago. Cancer."

"I'm so sorry to hear that."

"Well, just one of those things."

"And you haven't remarried?"

"Too busy between work and the boys. Greg was only nine at the time. And then there was my business and I guess, I guess I just wasn't ready or the right woman just wasn't around. I don't know. Just never seemed to be the right time to date."

"Until now?" Kate asked with a smile.

"Until now," Tom agreed. "What about you?"

"Oh, seems I've been divorced forever, longer than I was married. I remember back when I was struggling with the separation and pending divorce, reading how people live so long now that they hardly remember their first spouse. Never thought I would see that happen, but here I am, ten years later. I'm on friendly terms with Terri's dad. We don't fight. We get along. Just doesn't seem possible we were ever married, although Terri is proof of that. Is it that way for you?"

"Not really. Maybe because of her death. Sometimes I remember her as if it was just yesterday. In my memory she is always like she was before she died. I don't mean the sad times, through chemo and all. Before that. She never grew older or any different. But I have.”

“Grown older.”

“And changed. Want to walk?” Tom got up, placed some money down on their table and extended his hand to her.

“Sure, have to work off that dinner.”

They walked along the river-walk, dodging teens on skates and skateboards and stopping for a while to listen to music in the park as a local jazz band entertained.

“My company constructed this,” Tom mentioned.

“The river-walk?”

“Yes. Guess the city decided to go local this time. Usually they end up giving their construction work to bigger companies from other cities. But this wasn’t too complicated or too big. I saw it as a chance to give back to the city, a chance to help beautify the area. The gazebo too, we built. It was pretty easy.” They walked over to the gazebo and sat for a while as other couples walked through. Strains of music drifted through the air. Kate shivered as a breeze blew through.

“Cold?” Tom asked, putting an arm around her.

“Just a little. Guess it’s time to go,” she said getting up.

“You don’t have to work tomorrow?”

“No, but I’m tired. It’s been a long week and it’s time.”

They walked in silence back to his car. She wrapped her arm around his and felt the strength of his muscles. Someone to lean on, she thought.

He walked her to her door. She remembered all too well the awkwardness of saying goodnight on first dates. It had been a long time, but the memories came back.

“Thank you. I had a nice time,” she said, then added. “But don’t think this gets you off the hook as far as getting my house done on time. Don’t think I’m going to go easy on you just because we had dinner.”

“Wouldn’t think of it. In fact, I’d be disappointed if I didn’t get at least one complaint from you every day this week. Life would be so dull without that.” He paused awkwardly, leaned forward as if to kiss her. She reached out her hand and took his.

“Thank you, again.” She backed away. “Guess I’ll be seeing you.”

48

"That you will," he let go of her hand and watched as she entered her house. "Good night," he sighed as he walked back to his car.

What happened? She chided herself as she watched him pull away in his car, standing in her darkened kitchen. Why didn't she let him kiss her? Why hadn't he tried a little harder? She didn't know. It had been so awkward. This dating business doesn't get any easier. It was like being sixteen again but worse because she wasn't sixteen and should know better, be better at it by now. Had she just spoiled a good working relationship with a date? Had she just spoiled a potentially good relationship by her reluctance to kiss him?

She liked him and thought he liked her, but he may not realize she liked him. Will he ask her out again, or maybe she had to take the next step? Was she really ready to start dating again? Was he ready? What did one date hurt? Her mind was racing with so many questions, thoughts, just like in high school. Will he ask her out again? Did he like her? Did she like him? What would she tell Terri when Terri got home in two weeks? Why did she have to tell Terri anything?

Terri. In two weeks she'll be home. Tired though she was, Kate wasn't ready to go to sleep yet. She turned on the computer to check her email. A short message from Terri was there. It was bare bones, no meat to it.

"Work busy, lots of tables to clean up from summer golf tournaments. See you soon." Kate tried to read between the lines. It wasn't easy. Was she happy, enjoying herself, or was she homesick? If she was homesick, she could come home. She knew that, didn't she? But maybe she was too proud, too stubborn to come home. Terri was pretty stubborn, but if she wasn't happy she would have been quick to say something. She must be okay.

Damn, she missed her. Kate wished she were home. It was lonely in this empty house without her. What will I do when she goes to college, she wondered? Time enough to think about it when it happens. Kate pushed the thought out of her head. Maybe she'll go to a college nearby and come home on weekends? Or live at home and commute to school? Kate typed a breezy response to Terri's email telling about the work being done on the house.

"It's supposed to be done by the time you get home, but if not, one of the workers is cute and not too old. Hope you are having a good time. Don't work too much. Mom." She originally typed in "miss you," but decided against it. Sure she missed her but no sense bringing it up. She'll be home before she knew it. Two weeks.

Kate decided to visit a few more websites before going to bed. She checked out "Classmates," looking to see if any of her friends had registered. Their thirty-year reunion would be next year. It doesn't seem possible that many years had gone by. Too many. She wondered what her friends were doing, wondered if any of them would come to the reunion.

Then she clicked on the web search for Frank Shaughnessy. She knew it was probably foolish but she kept thinking maybe some more information would appear someday. She wished she could find an obituary just to confirm he was dead and make it real. She found it was hard to believe he could actually be gone. She wondered about her classmates: Were some of them dead as well? It all seemed so unreal.

She clicked on the page showing Frank's picture. He was so young. Surely he couldn't be gone. Maybe her dad had been mistaken, but Dad rarely was about these things. So sad, she thought. You never knew what life may bring or when it may end. Tom certainly knew that as well. She took one last look at Frank before closing out entirely from the Internet, shutting the computer off and going to bed.

"Bingo, Dad. Kathleen Connors is also Kathleen Jackson who grew up in Morenci. Seems she's been married and divorced and has one kid. How do you know her?" Chad emailed back to his dad.

How do I know her, Frank thought? How did I know her? How little I really knew her back then. Don't know her at all right now. Wonder why she's been searching the web for information on me, why now? Maybe I should send her an email. But now is not a good time. Will there ever be a good time? Obviously she must be wondering about me. He wondered about her. Married and divorced. So she's single. What did she look like after all these years? No, he couldn't just send an email. Maybe there's another

50

way. Maybe he could find out more about her first. He had some vacation time due him, maybe . . . But that was crazy.

"An old girlfriend. Can you get me any more information?" he emailed back to Chad.

"I don't know. I'm not exactly a dating service," Chad responded. Smart aleck, that son of mine, Frank thought, then read on. "I'll see what I can find. Or you could email her yourself."

Yes, I could, Frank thought.

At first Don refused to get involved. This was "her" thing, something she had to do. He stayed home and brooded, but gradually he started picking up the reams of paperwork, articles, copies of laws and books she had scattered throughout the house. Rather than make himself scarce when she had committee meetings, he had started by helping with coffee and sitting on the sidelines.

"Here, let me get that," he had told her as she prepared to bring coffee to her guests. "You need to be in there talking to your constituents. I can take care of this." He had pushed her back into the living room, then came in carrying a tray with coffee and coffee cups and a selection of cookies. He passed the tray around then sat it on the coffee table where guests could help themselves. When he saw that the pot was drained, he jumped up and went back into the kitchen to make more. Helen paused in her conversation, surprised by his actions.

After the meeting, while she saw her guests out, he picked up the coffee cups and cleaned the living room. He was busy putting dishes in the dish washer when she entered the kitchen.

"What are you doing?" she asked.

"What does it look like? I'm cleaning the kitchen. I do know my way around a kitchen."

"Yes, but you never did this before."

"I never had a future state representative as wife before either. Besides, after all you have done for me over the years, cooking, cleaning, entertaining business associates, raising our children, this is the least I can do. Let me help. You can rest or read up for tomorrow." He showed her out of the kitchen. She reluctantly went along with this.

"Oh, and tomorrow."

"Yes?"

"Why don't I drive you to your rally tomorrow night? That way you can relax and go over your notes before your speech."

"Okay, if you want to. Are you really okay with this?"

"With what?"

"The election and all."

"Well, if you can't beat them, join them."

"Oh, all right, I guess," she said as Don went back into the kitchen to finish up. She sat down, put her feet up and closed her eyes to rest her mind after a busy day and busier night. She had so much to think about, more than she could comprehend. But tomorrow would be another day.

Slowly Don found himself drawn into the conversations. He found himself enjoying the drives to meetings and rallies. Slowly, reluctantly, he found himself drawn into the excitement of the campaign till one morning he woke up and realized, much to his surprise, that he had become one of her strongest supporters.

And so it was with genuine happiness he toasted her after she received her party's nomination, winning the primary. Even though he knew it would mean more months of campaigning and yet another delay of his dream vacation, he was genuinely happy for her. She was genuinely surprised at him and found herself . . . in love again, if that were possible after all of those years.

The summer zoomed by much more quickly for Terri than she had expected. Bussing dishes hadn't been that terrible and in the process she had made some friends, and even more so, she had met Josh. She rode her bike back and forth to work each day. She would see him coming out of the pro-shop carrying a bag of golf clubs most days. He would smile and say, "Hi." The first time she met him she almost fell over her bike, but now she coolly said "hi," in response.

"Who is he?" she had asked the other bussers.

"That's Josh Baxter," Carolyn the hostess had told her. "But don't worry. He won't bother with the likes of you."

"Don't listen to her," a fellow busser with freckles and brown hair pulled up in a ponytail told her. "She just wants him for herself. He is dreamy, isn't he?" she added.

"Most definitely. Hi, I'm Terri," she introduced herself.

"I'm Sheri. You're new, aren't you?"

"That obvious?"

"No, it's just I know all of the other teens who work here and I didn't know you. I can show you the ropes."

"Thanks. I'd really appreciate it."

"So did you just move here or what?" Sheri asked in between showing her where to put dirty dishes and linens.

"Actually I'm spending the summer with my dad and stepmom. I'm from Ohio."

"That's too bad. After a couple of months of bussing tables you could graduate to hostess. That's what I'm hoping for."

"I should be long gone by then." Sheri showed her the ins and outs of clearing away dishes, how to stack them, where to put them. "Thank you so much," Terri said when they finished. "Maybe you could come over to my house some time."

"Sure. That would be fun. See you tomorrow."

Josh was so dreamy. She hadn't thought so at first, cute yes, but not dreamy. Then there had been the night of the beach party towards the end of the summer. They had kissed under the moonlight. It had been so perfect. She hadn't expected it. They had been walking and talking and next she knew they were kissing. That was when she knew she had to come back. She had to go to school there in California just to see if this went anywhere. Not that he had said anything to encourage her to stay. He was just himself, so nice, so sweet, so dreamy.

She thought about that kiss the whole flight home. Where she had been reluctant to leave her friends at home for California, now she was reluctant to leave California. She resented having to come home. It would be good to see her friends, but not so good to see her mom, unless her mom agreed to her going back. After that she would be glad to see her even as she prepared to leave her again.

V

He was running, running, running. From what, he didn't know. He just knew he couldn't stop or it would catch him. Down familiar hallways, through the same tunnel. He knew how it would end.

He awoke with a start, shooting straight up in bed, waking his sleeping bedmate.

"Another bad dream?" she mumbled, tumbling over.

"Yes," he said, still sitting straight up.

"Is it the same one?" she reached over to touch his back in a half-hearted, sleep-deprived effort to give comfort. She knew the routine. It was getting old.

"Yes, go back to sleep," he told her, slipping his legs over the side of the bed.

"Where are you going?" she asked.

"I'm just getting up for a few minutes. Go back to sleep." She gladly accepted his permission to get a few more hours of sleep before the alarm clock woke her for the day. A more devoted girlfriend would maybe get up with him, sit with him, talk to him, but she had been there before. She knew the routine. It was a familiar one. There really wasn't much she could do. She could get up and then spend the rest of her day in a sleep-deprived haze, or go back to sleep and wake up well rested, ready to begin her day. Why should both of them be exhausted? She knew he didn't want to talk anyway. He wanted to be alone with his thoughts and so she gave him what he said he wanted and went back to sleep.

Kevin got up, looked at the clock, two o'clock. Damn. If it had been four o'clock he would have just started a pot of coffee and got some work done. There were lesson plans to go over as he prepared for another school year. But it was way too early for that. If he went back to bed he would probably toss and turn for an or hour or two, keeping Allyson awake before falling asleep for a few precious hours until the alarm went off. He hated this. What to do?

He went into the second bedroom that had been turned into a den/office for him to do school work at night, sat in the overstuffed chair and tried to sink back into sleep. When that didn't happen he went to his desk, sat down, reached into the second drawer where he kept his notebook and proceeded to write.

"I have bad dreams," he wrote. His character was a science teacher by day, detective, solver of mysteries by night.

"I have bad dreams," he told his youthful assistant, the family dog he had inherited along with this drafty old house when his grandfather, his sole living relative, had passed away. "But what's different from other people's bad dreams, is that mine come true, in some shape or form," he informed his attentive listener, who wagged his tale in anticipation of a doggie treat.

By day, John was a mild-mannered seventh grade science teacher; by night he used his knowledge of science to assist in solving local mysteries . . . Kevin wrote. "Little did his students know his dual identity. No one suspected."

No one suspected that the mild-mannered, third-grade teacher had a secret life, that of a mystery writer. By day, Kevin taught in a local elementary school, one of only two men on staff. The work was routine, yet never the same. He was one of the few male role models available to his students, many of whom came from single-parent families. He felt terribly young to take on the collective identity of substitute father to a room of twenty-two students, especially since he was not a father himself and his relationship with his own father was anything but close. So he lived the life of a quiet, elementary school teacher by day light, but by night he was plagued by dreams, good and bad, always exciting.

His longing for adventure spilled out into his dreams and onto paper rather than invade his day-to-day existence. He needed to be stable, calm, steadfast, predictable and just as a teacher. In his dreams he could be wild, moody, prone to rash decisions, a risk taker, adventurer extraordinaire, all without leaving the comfort of his bed. He had a dual identity much like super-heroes of comic book fame: Peter Parker and Spiderman, Clark Kent and Superman. He was not Peter Parker, but in his dreams he was another 007 James Bond, solving international crimes, leading a life of intrigue and danger, filled with many beautiful women. Or he could be another Sherlock Holmes, solving crimes for Scotland Yard.

It was all good, harmless fun, except that he had bad dreams, recurring bad dreams. Allyson had encouraged him to see a shrink. Super-heroes don't go to shrinks, he told himself.

"I'm fine," he told Allyson.

"Okay, if you say so, but I'm not the one waking up at two o'clock every night because of some dream about the bogey monster."

"It's not a bogey monster."

"Whatever."

"No, it's always somewhat the same. It starts out in some exotic setting or maybe a glamorous party or high adventure, but it always ends up with me being chased, sometimes falling, sometimes I wake up before I fall."

"Sounds like something to talk to a shrink about, but what do I know?"

She was right about that. What did she know, Kevin thought? She could be so annoying, with her legal mind and affidavits and quid pro quo. He didn't know why he put up with her, except that she put up with him. She was gorgeous and put up with him. How many women would put up with him? He could think of maybe two in his life time, one of those being his mother. The other was his college girlfriend. What had happened to her, he wondered. They had been good together. Oh, yeah, she went into the Peace Corps. He had said he would wait, but two years was a long time to be alone, and then he had met Allyson.

Allyson with her big smile and way of laughing at all his jokes, even when they weren't funny. Had it been a show to get his attention? No, Allyson was too genuine for that. She could have had any one of those high class lawyers she worked with, but she chose to go out with him. He wondered why.

"Because you make me laugh," she had said. "I need laughter in my life. Do you know how often a typical lawyer laughs during the day?"

"Two or three times but it's always that evil laugh as they tweak their mustaches."

She laughed. "See, that's why I go out with you. Aside from those evil laughs, we don't get a lot of laughs on a typical day. At

56

least I don't. It's nice to go out with someone outside of my office, outside of the world of law, have a drink, talk about normal stuff, and laugh."

And so she had laughed her way into his bed and into his heart; and his former girlfriend … what was her name? … anyway, she had fallen in love with another volunteer in the Peace Corps and they were now living on plankton and rice and whatever it is they eat in those third world countries. Meanwhile, he was teaching third grade, living in relative luxury with a rich (comparatively speaking that is–it doesn't take much to be rich in comparison to what a beginning teacher makes) girlfriend, room-mate, soul-mate, whatever.

Life was good except that he had bad dreams. Rather than psychoanalyze them away, he had decided to use them as fodder for writing, an escape he had learned in high school when he would hear his parents' fighting. He would drown out the noise with music and escape into a world of fantasy through books and writing. Perhaps that was why he had chosen to teach grade school, unlike most males who opted for the older grades, considering the nurturing of small children women's work. When he had been in grade school, life had been good; then the fighting began and then when the fighting had ended his dad moved out. He knew how much he missed having a man around.

Perhaps he was stunted mentally at a grade school level and that's why he related so well to this age group. He supposed a shrink would help him sort all of this out, free him of troubling dreams, help him grow up and teach high school, maybe coach a sport like any self-respecting man, but he didn't know that he wanted to be cured. Perhaps the cure would be worse than the illness.

He was content with his dreams, content with being a third-grade teacher, at least for now. He wanted to be left alone with his neurosis. He wasn't hurting anyone and outside of losing some sleep, he was still a facsimile of a good teacher, maybe even the genuine article, and he had his writing to feed his fantasies, allow him to escape. What more could an ordinary, neurotic man of twenty-six ask for?

"So when are you and Allyson going to get married?" Oooops, well it seemed everyone expected it. His mother, her parents, their friends. "I'd like to have grandchildren before I die, while I'm still around to enjoy them," his mother prodded.

Yes, Mom, but didn't she see he had children a-plenty in his life already, a classroom full of them. He was still a child himself. He couldn't raise a child just yet, not till he dealt with his bad dreams, which he wasn't willing to deal with, and so he prolonged his own childhood a little longer.

"What do you do when you get up in the middle of the night?" Allyson asked.

"I told you, sometimes I do lesson plans, sometimes I grade papers, sometimes I write."

"What are you writing? Let me see."

"No, it's nothing. It's not something for anyone to see yet."

"But when it's ready, you'll let me read it, won't you?"

"You'll be the first and probably the only one to read it." This seemed to satisfy her, but only for a while.

"What is it about?" she asked two weeks later.

"What is what about?"

"The book you're writing, what is it about?"

"That again. A murder mystery."

"Then you'll need a good lawyer to help you with the legal details and the crime scene."

"I'll be sure to let you know if I need that."

"Come on, let me read it. You've been working on it for so long. Let me help."

"No, I'm not ready. It's not ready to be read by anyone. Just go to work, do whatever it is you lawyers do all day."

The remaining two weeks went by quicker than Kate expected. She continued on friendly terms with Tom, calling him almost every day. Still the house wasn't done on time. The kitchen was in disarray. The old walls had been knocked down, leaving the new ones in place with a covering of plaster all over everything. The plastic sheets that had been laid down to protect appliances and cupboards hadn't caught all of the dust. The new floor had not yet been laid, but it looked like finally all the plumbing was in place. Most of what remained was clean up and finish work.

"One more week," Tom had assured her.

They had gone out several times since that first date. It was still awkward. She enjoyed his company, just wasn't sure. Where was it going? Were they just two friends who happened to be lonely, or was there more? She preferred to think of him as a friend, but other thoughts came popping up at times. Just wait till all of this mess was done, she told herself. It was too awkward trying to have a friendship and a business relationship. Maybe when they were finished she'd know whether this was just a passing fancy. Maybe it was just because she was missing Terri. Terri would be home soon. The house will be back together and time will tell.

The summer had gone by more quickly than she had thought possible. She had been busy at work, busy with the house and of course there was Tom. She had had little time to worry about being lonely except for those Friday and Saturday evenings lying awake in her bed. The occasional night out with her friends and the dates with Tom didn't fill up the time between two and four when her mind would race. Still, overall it had been a pleasant summer. She had saved her vacation time to use during the school year, once Terri got home.

August fifteenth already, she thought to herself as she drove to the airport. She had taken the following week off from work for school shopping with Terri and just catching up. The few phone calls and brief emails she had received over the summer were hardly adequate to fill her in on all the nuances of teen life. They had never been separated for this long before. She and Terri's dad had been divorced for more than ten years, separating when Terri was just five. It had been a relatively amiable separation and divorce, for Terri's sake as well as for all their sakes.

Kate remembered again how back then when overwhelmed by feelings of guilt, conflict, anger and grief over the end of her marriage, she had read how people live many lifetimes now. You forget all about your first marriage with the passage of time. It hadn't seemed possible at the time, but now it was true. The years she and Dick had had together were so short in comparison to her total span of years. It was hard to remember why they even married and why they broke up. Their lives had drifted so far apart over the years. They were amicable strangers who shared a daughter.

When Dick had remarried a few years ago and then relocated to California last year, Kate had not been sure how to take it. Dick had been good in the past, helping with Terri. They had worked out their own custody arrangement, outside of the courts — one that worked for them. Dick had been supportive of her going to school to get her MSW, keeping Terri on nights she had classes and extra nights to give her time for homework.

It had still been a struggle, but his support had helped make it possible. She wasn't sure what she thought about him moving so far away. She got along with his new wife and Terri got along with her as well as her two children. But now they had to work out a different arrangement. No more having weekends off while Terri was at her dad's. And what about holidays? Terri wouldn't be able to spend Christmas Eve at her dad's anymore and Christmas morning with her. Still Terri was old enough to decide a few things by herself. She had wanted to spend the summer with her dad and that was okay with her. She would have her the rest of the year.

Terri was strangely subdued when Kate picked her up. That's all right, Kate told herself. That's natural after two months away. She couldn't expect them to just pick up where they had left off. She needs some time to readjust. Just give her a little time, she had told herself.

"So, how was your summer?"

"Okay."

"Just okay? Did you meet anybody nice?"

"Well, actually there was this one guy."

"Really, tell me about him."

"There's not much to tell. He suggested I stay and go to school out there."

"And what did you tell him?"

"I told him my mom would freak if I even suggested it."

"Right you are," Kate agreed.

"But, you know Mom, they have a really good high school not far from Dad and Janet's house. Really nice, and I met some of the kids in my grade. They were great."

"You are not really suggesting this, are you?"

"See, I knew you would freak. Can't we even talk about it?"

"We can talk, but the answer is no. What would I do without you to keep me in line and give me grief?"

"The same thing you did all summer. The same thing you do all year. Work. You've got your work. You don't need me around."

"That's not true. Look, let's not discuss this anymore tonight. You just got back. Let's just give it a rest for now, okay?"

"Whatever," Terri said and maintained an icy silence the rest of the way home despite any attempts at small talk by Kate. She made a bee-line for the computer the minute she got home and spent the rest of her first night back talking to her new friends in between a short break for dinner.

"Not how I had imagined her first night back," Kate thought to herself. "Not at all." Was this how it had been when Frank had suggested to his parents that he stay with his grandparents for his senior year? Of course, they were going to say no. Why would they say yes? At least Terri has email to keep in touch with her boyfriend. All they had had was snail mail, which he had not been good about sending. The phone hadn't really been an option. What chance had they had? With the internet it's much easier to maintain a long distance relationship now. She didn't even know this guy's name. She didn't know anything about him.

"Terri?" she hesitantly approached her daughter as she punched at the keyboard.

"Yeah, what?"

"Tell me some more about this guy," Kate said and sat down next to the computer.

"Oh," Terri turned away from the monitor, "There's really not much to tell."

"What's his name? How old is he? How did you meet? I want to know."

"Well," Terri began slowly, "His name's Josh Baxter. He's seventeen and works as a caddy at the golf course by dad's house. That's where I met him. He's real sweet, not like the guys around here." Terri began and slowly the events of the summer spilled out.

"But it isn't just about him, Mom. It's about me and California and new beginnings. I'm different there."

"I know it must be hard to come back to dull old Ohio after a really great summer. It's hard to return to the old routine."

"But why do I have to? Why can't I make a fresh start in a new place, a place I really like with people I like?"

"What about your friends here?"

"I can still see them when I'm here. I won't be gone forever. I'll come home for Christmas and spring break and other times."

"What does your dad think about this? Have you talked to him about it?"

"He's fine with it, and Janet too. They said it was up to you."

Great, Kate thought. Leaving it up to me to be the bad guy.

"Let me think about it. We can talk some more tomorrow," Kate told her and went to her room, leaving Terri in the glow of the computer monitor.

"Can we meet for lunch?" Kate called Tom on the phone.

"But I thought you would be spending the day with Terri?" Tom responded.

"No, seems she has other plans, ones that don't include me."

"Sounds like your typical teenager. Sure, I can get away for a while this afternoon."

"Thanks," Kate said once they had agreed upon a place and time to meet. She had to talk to someone about Terri. She knew it was a done deal, but she still needed to talk. She had already talked with Terri's father, and he was okay with her moving there, as Terri had already informed her. He thought it was a good idea. Now it was up to her. Terri had made plans to see her friends today so that meant she had the whole day to herself to brood about the situation. She didn't want to brood entirely alone.

They sat in silence through most of their lunch. Kate picked at her food. She knew she had to eat, but nothing tasted good to her right now.

"So, what's up?" Tom finally broke the silence.

"Nothing's up. Does something have to be up for me to ask you out to lunch?"

"No, but you are obviously not interested in eating. Something must be bothering you. It's Terri, isn't it?"

Kate paused before answering. "She wants to move to California with her dad."

"Oh," Tom leaned back in his seat, contemplating what Kate had said. "And that would be . . . bad?"

"Bad? It would be horrible. I'll miss her junior and senior years in high school. All those important events. I'll miss them all."

"You'll also miss staying up at night worrying when she will come home."

"You think I won't worry just because she's no longer living in my house?" Kate snapped, "I thought you'd be more sympathetic. I thought you'd understand. How would you have felt if your sons had moved out while still in high school?"

"I guess I'd have to give that one a thought. They were basically good kids; still, high school . . . Those were some pretty stressful years. I don't regret them now, but still . . . You'd have so much more free time to spend with me."

"You're no help at all. I should have known better," Kate took her napkin out of her lap and prepared to get up.

"Wait," Tom reached out and placed his hand on hers. "Wait, I'm sorry. I'm not the best listener, I guess."

"More than guess."

"Give me another try. How about if I say, that's terrible. Of course Terri can't move all the way across the country to live with her father, leaving you all alone. How could she think of it?"

"You're not being helpful."

"Then what do you want me to say?"

"You don't have to say anything. Can you just listen?"

"I'm trying. Is it that you think it wouldn't be good for Terri to live with her father?"

"No, actually it might be good for her to live with her dad for a while. Give them more time to get to know each other. It's just," Kate paused before starting again. "It's just that I'm not ready. I'm not ready to let her go. Sure she was gone all summer, but that was only two months. Sure I knew this day would come eventually, but not just yet. I thought I had two more years to get used to the idea of her being gone. But how can I compete with California and the nice house with a pool. How can I compete with all her dad can give her?"

"It's hard to let our kids go," Tom said, taking her hand.

"But, I guess I have to," Kate said. "It's just too soon." Tom sat in silence with her.

"You still got me," Tom broke the silence, "and you got the holidays. She'll have to stay with you over the holidays."

"I know. I know."

"So what are you going to do?"

"What can I do? I guess I've got to let her go. I can't hold her back, can I?"

"Oh, you could try, but think about a whole year living with a very angry teenager. And maybe she'll change her mind after a couple of months."

"I don't want her to do that. If she's going to do this, I want her to give it a good try. At least complete one semester, but maybe after that . . ." Kate tried to smile. "It will be good for her. And it's not like she's living with a complete stranger. Her dad can look after her. It might be good for both of them."

"So, it's settled?" Tom asked.

"Oh, I guess it was settled before I even knew anything about it. I know what I have to do. And maybe it won't be so bad."

"Maybe you'll find time for all those things you always wanted to do but couldn't because of being a parent."

"And what do you know about that?"

"Plenty, because I'm still not doing them. Things like going away for the weekend whenever you want. Traveling, catching up on your sleep, taking care of yourself for a change."

"And why aren't you doing these things?"

"Maybe because I hadn't found the right person to do some of this with," Tom said with a smile.

"Oh no, that sounds way too serious to me. I can only handle one situation at a time. First I have to consider Terri."

"And when will you consider Kate?"

"I will, I always do, you just may not realize it," Kate said as she stood up. "Thanks for listening anyway. Lunch is on me today," she said as she picked up the bill to pay at the register.

"Let me know how it all works out," Tom got up and walked with her to her car.

"Sure I will. I'll call you," Kate said as she got in her car and drove away. I will call you, just not right away, Kate thought to herself. He sounded like he wanted to be more serious than she was right now. Time enough to sort all of this out when Terri was gone. When she was gone, not if. Kate knew what she had to do.

To pray is to dream in league with God.
Rabbi Abraham Heschel

VI

The two weeks before Terri left for California were both the best and most difficult days she could remember. They spent time shopping, picking out a wardrobe for California, finalizing details about the school year. Her dad took care of registering her at her new high school. Terri was more agreeable than she had been in a long time. She even allowed her to fuss over her a bit. Not too much, but some. It was a crumb she tossed to her mother.

Kate arrived home after seeing Terri off at the airport, weary and yet unable to relax. She had made Terri promise she would be home for Thanksgiving and Christmas and repeatedly asked her to call her, or at least email her. She wondered how much good that would really do once she got settled in California and was spending time with her new friends. Still she had had to make the attempt.

She fixed herself a snack and turned on the computer. Certainly it was too soon for email from Terri; still you never knew what might show up. Her heart leapt into her throat when she saw she had a message from a flyboy56. Who could that be? She prepared to delete it as spam but stopped. … Flyboy? Shaugnessy? Couldn't be. Not her Frank. This must be a bad joke. She clicked on the screen.

"Hi Katy, remember me? We dated eons ago, while in high school."

This must be a cruel joke. Maybe he was mistaken. Maybe there was another Frank Shaughnessy.

She replied, "I thought you were dead." She paused before hitting the send button. It sounded so harsh, but she couldn't think of any other way to say it. Best to just get it out there in the open. She checked her other email then jumped when she received an answer to her email.

"He must be at his computer right now," she thought to herself. "If only I knew how to use instant messenger. If only I had paid more attention when Terri had tried to teach me how to do it." She clicked on his response.

"No, I assure you, I am quite alive and well, unless there is another Frank Shaughnessy who dated Kate Jackson in Morenci in 1973. My dad died eighteen years ago, though, Frank Sr."

It had to be him. There couldn't be two of him.

"So sorry. I had heard about your dad. How did you find me?"

"Seems you've been trying to find me. Your name showed up at the Aviation journal web site a number of times." Oh no, Kate thought. How embarrassing.

"But how do I know you are Frank and not just somebody pretending to be Frank?" She waited for his reply.

"Remember our first date? We played tennis and then sat on the park bench and talked for hours. Remember sailing at my grandparent's cottage, getting stuck in a small canal, getting sunburned? Do you remember when I first kissed you? I do. In my grandparent's car, before we said goodnight. I backed the car into the driveway, then when you looked back at your house, I slipped over next to you. Need I say more?"

Boy, he's good. If he's not Frank, it was someone who knew a lot about both of us. Kate stared at the screen for a long time. She wasn't sure what to do. She didn't have to answer right away. She could wait, give herself some time to adjust to this information, or she could email back.

"Is that really you, Frank? I can't believe it. What are doing now? How are you? Tell me about yourself." Kate sent the email and waited expectantly for a response. When one didn't come after fifteen minutes she decided it was time to turn off the computer and go to bed. Perhaps he got called away or something. Frank never was too good at correspondence. Kate remembered the long waits for letters that never came. Maybe this is just a repeat of that, she thought. Or maybe . . . who knew what. Best not to spend too much time worrying about it, she told herself and went to bed.

What am I doing, Frank asked himself. Now that he had made contact with Kate, he wasn't sure what to do. Was this really a good idea? He wasn't really a free man. Sure he wasn't married, but the military during times of war . . .? Might as well be married, he thought. He wasn't free to just come and go. How much could

66

he tell her? Not where he was or what his mission entailed. He had spent a good part of the last year in Afghanistan, helping to locate rebel forces and seeking out terrorists. His knowledge of the Middle East from Desert Storm had been a tremendous asset.

Now he was involved in something bigger, more plans for the Middle East. He had been flown back stateside in order to take part in strategic planning. Sure, the U.S. was not involved in a full-scale war just yet, but war was war. Call it what you will in the states, for those on the front-line it was still a war. For security reasons he couldn't tell Kate any of this. What should he tell her? What could he tell her? Was this a good idea or just craziness?

Kate was disappointed the next night when there was still no email from flyboy56. What was she thinking anyway? As if they could start up from where they left off or something. Crazy idea. Still she was curious about him. Was he married? What about his son? She was about to sign off when a message popped into her inbox. It was from Terri.

"Hi, Mom. Just wanted to let you know I got here okay and I'm settling in. Can't wait for school to start. Thank you so much. Love, Terri."

Now that was different. How unlike Terri. Thanking her and telling her she loved her. Not that she never did those things, but they weren't a common occurrence. Terri saved up her kind words, usually for special occasions or when she wanted something.

"Glad to hear you are settling in. Good luck on your first day of school. Let me know if there is anything I can do. Love, Mom." Now there was something to take her mind off of Frank. Something much more important than any of the men in her life – Terri.

She sent her email and was preparing to log off when she received a message from Frank.

"Sorry about not responding to your questions last night. I got called away," he lied. Well, it wasn't entirely a lie. He had called himself away. "I'm fine. I'm divorced. I followed my father's footsteps into the military, as apparently you know. I have one son, Chad. He also went into the military. What about you?"

Kate knew that would be coming. What should she say? That she was divorced, had one daughter and felt her life was over. Yeah, right. Just what he wanted to hear.

"I'm fine. I'm divorced too. My daughter is spending the year with her dad in California. She just left yesterday but already I'm going crazy without her . . ." no, delete that last part. "You must be very proud of your son." There. That tells him about as much as he told her. She clicked the send button and powered off the computer.

Kate walked through the house alone. It seemed so much emptier this time than when Terri had left for the summer. Of course that had just been for a short time. Kate had been prepared for that. She had spent the summer getting the house ready for Terri's return. How ironic. The house was done just before Terri left again. Nothing had prepared her for this. She finally had two bathrooms, but no one to share them with. What good were two bathrooms to her? One advantage, at least now she didn't have to go downstairs in the middle of the night when she woke up and nature called. It wasn't a complete waste, she told herself. And it increased the value of the house. Still, the house was so empty.

She was startled by the sound of the phone ringing through the empty house.

"Hi, are you okay?" Tom's familiar voice sounded over the line.

"I guess so. The house is so empty."

"Do you want company?" he asked.

"No, I've got to get used to the quiet. I might as well start tonight. Thanks for asking."

"You know how to reach me if you change your mind."

Change my mind? I have changed my mind — about Terri. This was insane. I never should have agreed to it. What was she thinking? What had she been thinking to let her go? But she had let her go. Can't change that now. Just have to make the best of it, Kate told herself.

Stupid, stupid, stupid. How could she have been so stupid to think Josh was really interested in her? And here she was, miles from home, stuck for the whole school year. What had she been thinking?!

Sheri had followed her out of the school yard. Terri's face was burning as if she had been slapped, burning from embarrassment. Josh had hardly looked at her when she said hi, had hardly acknowledged her existence.

"You okay?" Sheri asked.

"Yeah, no, I'm not. Josh hardly even said hi to me. He looked right through me as if I didn't exist."

"Maybe it wasn't a good time for him. You know, we're all back at school. Maybe he just wanted a chance to catch up with his old friends. Besides, as far as he knew, you had gone home for the school year and weren't coming back."

"Yeah, I saw him catching up with Caroline."

"It doesn't mean anything. They used to date, but that was way in the past, like a year ago. She's history. He's just being nice."

"Maybe you're right. Maybe I should just talk to him, find out where I stand and all."

"Yeah, but you can't do it from here and if we are late we'll both get detentions."

"Yeah, right," Terri reassured herself as she walked back across the school parking lot with Sheri. Besides she had better things to worry about than Josh Baxter right now. She had a whole new school to learn to navigate. She had just been thrown off when she saw him, she told herself.

It was several weeks before Terri had a chance to talk to Josh. Being a senior, he wasn't in any of her classes. The days had been filled with learning the ropes, new school, new teachers, new possible friends. She had also signed up for yearbook, hoping to gain access to the school dark room to develop her pictures. She had taken photography classes at her old high school and thought she had some knack for taking photos. She liked the dark room, the smell of chemicals and seeing blank sheets transform into pictures before her eyes. It was quickly becoming a lost art, with the prevalence of digital cameras, which made it all the more fascinating to her.

Besides, she reminded herself, spending her junior year here hadn't been just about Josh, although he did fall into the equation. She decided to focus on school, photography and her new life here, until she bumped into Josh once again, knocking her books out of her arms.

"Why don't you watch where you are . . ." she started to say until she looked up and saw Josh bending down to help her pick up her books. "Josh, hi," she stammered.

"Sorry, crowded hallway and all, didn't see you."

"That's okay. How are you?"

"I'm great, what about you? I thought you had to go home to Ohio for school?"

"Oh, that. Things changed."

Josh looked around the crowded hallway, "Can we talk?"

"Sure," she responded.

"Not now. Maybe after school. Could you meet me outside of the track?"

Terri started to say she had yearbook, then thought better of it and said, "Sure."

"Great. See you then," Josh said as he left.

"What are you grinning about?" Sheri asked as she came upon her a few minutes later.

"Josh wants to meet me after school," she pulled her aside and whispered.

"No way," Sheri responded.

"Way," Terri said as they walked to class, giggling.

Josh was in his running clothes when he found her. "I've just got a few minutes. I need to warm up and run a couple miles."

"That's okay. I've got yearbook committee."

"You do? That's great," he said then paused awkwardly. "Look, you know about this summer."

"Yes," Terri said anxiously, not sure where this was going but suspecting it wasn't where she had hoped.

"I just . . . I didn't want you to get the wrong idea. I mean, I like you and all, but it's not like we were even dating."

"What are you talking about?"

"I mean, you deciding to go to school here. I thought you were leaving after the summer. And now, here you are. It was just one kiss. One kiss and you're moving across the country . . ."

"Is that what you think? You think I decided to go to school here this year because of you."

"Didn't you?"

"Of all the conceit. Did it ever occur to you my dad lives here and I might like to have some time with him? Like I would completely rearrange my life for you?"

"Oh, okay, so you didn't. Good, that's great then. I just didn't want there to be any misunderstanding and all. I'm sorry. My mistake. So we're still friends. We still work together. I didn't want it to be awkward."

"Sure, friends. Now go and run. I have a meeting to get to." Terri watched him run off to join the rest of the cross country team. "It's not awkward at all," she said to herself as she walked home.

"Terri, where were you, or need I ask? Were you with Josh? Is that why you skipped yearbook? Tell me all the details," Sheri insisted as she opened the door to Terri's room. Terri was lying on her bed, staring at her homework.

"There's nothing to tell," Terri said.

"But what did he say?"

"He was worried that I had moved here because of him . . . I told him no."

"Well, didn't you?"

"But he doesn't need to know that, especially if he doesn't feel the same way about me. Besides it wasn't just about him."

"Keep telling yourself that."

"It wasn't. It's a new adventure being here. It's just that Josh was part of the adventure."

"Maybe he could still be. He didn't completely blow you off, did he?"

"No, he said we could be friends."

"Oh, no, the f-word. He blew you off."

"We can be friends, though. Just see. I'm going to focus on my schoolwork, my photography and my new best friend."

"Me?"

"No one else. Now, please let me study." When Sheri left, Terri wrote in her journal. "What a fool I was. Why, why did I move here?" She contemplated calling her mom to see if she could come home but was pretty sure she knew what the answer would be. Her mom would say she needs to give it a fair chance.

"I'll just have to hang tough," she told herself, flopping on her back, clutching her journal to her chest and staring at the ceiling.

Now came the hard part. Having won the primary and her husband's heart, now she needed to win the election in this predominantly Democratic county. Why her party had picked her, she didn't know. She just knew she was going to do her best regardless of the outcomes.

After the primary the real work began. There had been no strong candidate competing against her, just two who had decided to test the waters by throwing their hats into the ring, much as she had. But apparently she had been the stronger candidate. The work before the primary had been important in terms of laying the groundwork for the rest of the campaign. Now she was running against an incumbent in a strongly Democratic area of the state. The one thing she had in her favor was the downturn in the economy which tended to make voters ready for change. Why else would they even consider a relative unknown?

Despite her years on the school board and other volunteer activities, she was still a relative unknown. She had never sought the lime light, preferring to quietly do the work that needed to be done behind the scenes, not seeking recognition or honor. Her reward was in a job well done. All of this had to change. No shrinking violet or wall-flower would be elected to congress. She needed to get her name and face out in the public. She needed public recognition and she needed it fast.

What she had thought to be a fast pace before the primary, now seemed like a leisurely stroll. Every minute of her life was scheduled, jammed full of meetings, press conferences, public appearances. If not for the support of her husband, she didn't know how she would have done it. Despite all her experience as a teacher in speaking in front of groups and handling questions, she found the almost constant being "on," the sound-bites and living under the magnifying glass of public scrutiny exhausting and yet in some ways exhilarating.

She felt young again, like when she was in college working on the campaign of a senator as a volunteer. Then she had been a Democrat, Don a staunch Republican. She wasn't sure how it had happened that they ended up together. They had started out fighting, on different sides of the issues, but they found common ground. She hadn't agreed with everything the Democratic Party had stood for. She had supported their stand on poverty issues, but not on abortion. She had agreed with some of their policies but not always. It wasn't that far a step from a moderate Democrat to a moderate Republican. And Don had changed too over the years, not staunchly following the Republican Party line, not being afraid to be independent.

And so it had come to this. She never would have imagined as a young girl of twenty that she would someday not only marry a Republican, but become one herself and run for Congress on the Republican ticket. It had been a long journey to this space in time. So she kissed babies, shook hands, walked for miles, talked even more, all on the campaign trail.

She enjoyed meeting with her constituents, small business owners, young mothers who escaped their houses by volunteering for a few hours a week, much as she had, young and old, alike. She met with them all. Idealistic college students, much as she had been, much as her former students had been.

The campaign office was quietly bustling. Volunteers were stuffing flyers in one room, others were making phone calls, contacting voters, soliciting their support. She sat down at a desk, removed her shoes and rubbed her feet. It had been a grueling morning, a press conference and reception she had been invited to attend with other Republican candidates but requiring her standing all morning in her good, high-heeled shoes.

"So what's on the schedule this afternoon?" she asked her manager.

"A luncheon meeting with local business owners to discuss the problems of downtown businesses, followed by a rally at city hall. Tonight you have that fund-raiser at the Commonwealth Center, formal attire."

"Will my chauffeur be picking me up?"

"Yes, your husband will be by around 5:30 p.m. to pick you up. He'll also bring your black dress."

"What would I do without you," she said as she drank bottled water.

"Oh, did you see the latest polls? You are edging your way up, 36 percent."

“Good, but not good enough.”

“It’s still better than the Republican candidate in the last election. You may actually have a shot.”

“Of course I do, or why would I be running?”

“Well, you know, some people say we have no chance against Thompson, no matter who we run against him. This election is more about preparing for the next election when his seat is open.”

“Well, we’ll see about that. Who are those people anyway? Must be Democrats.”

“Actually political analysts, if you must know, but you’ve already done better in the polls than those same analysts had predicted.”

“Thanks for the vote of confidence,” Helen said with a laugh. She knew from the start she was a long shot; still, it was unnerving to hear this from her own campaign manager. Somehow along the way she had begun to believe she could do it. “All the more reason to work that much harder.”

“You know, there’s a point where all of the hard work in the world won’t win you an election.”

“It almost sounds like you are trying to soften the blow. We haven’t lost yet.”

“No, just reminding you so you take care of yourself in the process.”

“That’s what I have Don and you for, to take care of me while I win this election,” Helen responded with false bravado. Who was she kidding, she told herself. She knew very well that all of the work in the world won’t win an election. Sometimes it is just a matter of being in the right place at the right time, being the right candidate when people are ready for a change and having the right people on your side working for you. She certainly had the right people on her staff, all dedicated, hard-working, but was this the right place at the right time? She guessed she would find out when the polls closed and the votes were tallied.

“Mr. Peters, Mr. Peters, the toilet in the boys’ bathroom is broken again. There’s water everywhere,” two former students came running in.

He didn't know why he always was the one they called on for such an emergency. He'd have to go to the front office and ask for the maintenance man, same as the female staff. He stopped another teacher in the hallway and asked her to get maintenance then proceeded to the boys' bathroom. One of the urinals was squirting water, much to the delight of a crowd of boys.

"Okay, okay, everybody stand back. Don't you have places to go?"

"It's recess."

"Then go outside. The show's over."

They reluctantly left the room. Kevin tried to sneak up on the urinal to see if he could stop the flow of water without getting soaked himself. He was relieved when he jiggled the handle successfully and stopped the spray of water; but then he slipped and fell in the puddle of water when he turned to leave. He heard a round of laughter from students who had returned and were hiding by the stalls as the janitor arrived.

"About time you got here," he said, picking himself up, water all up and down the side of his pants and shirt. He looked over at the laughing students. "I thought I told you to leave," he started to say, then laughed and slipped his way across the room to the paper towels.

"You looked so funny, Mr. Peters," the boys continued to laugh.

"I know, I know. Next time can't you get another teacher to come?"

"They all tell us to get you," they replied.

He was still wet when he arrived home. He was surprised to see Allyson's car already parked in the parking spot for their apartment.

"Allyson," he called as he entered. "What are you doing here? Are you sick or something?" He found her sitting in his den with his manuscript in front of her. She jumped up as he came in.

"Kevin, I love it. It still needs some work on the details, but I love it. What happened to you?" she asked.

"Oh, toilet emergency again, like pretty much every week. It's just that usually I'm able to change my clothes before you get home. You loved it? You loved what?" he asked as the answer sunk in. "My book? How could you do this? I told you it wasn't ready. How could you . . . You loved it?"

"Yes, it's great. You should get it published."

"Whoa, slow down. It's not even finished yet."

"But it's almost done. I bet I could get a publisher to look at it. There's that publishing house my firm does business with. I bet I could get someone from there to look at it."

"Whoa, too fast. You really think it's good? You really think it's ready to be seen by a publisher? Wait, why are you home?"

"I came home early. Sorry, sweetie," she said as she came closer. "I just couldn't stand the suspense anymore. I was so curious. I knew if I waited for you to be ready, I might never get to read it. I was just going to look at it, not read it all the way through, but once I got started I couldn't put it down. Do you forgive me?"

"No, yes, you went behind my back. How can I trust you not to be sneaking into all of my stuff any time I'm not around . . . You really liked it?"

"I swear, Kevin, it was the first time I ever did something like this. I've never gone through your stuff before. I didn't look at anything else. How does it end?"

"Not sure yet."

"They catch the crook, of course, don't they? I mean they always catch the crook in murder mysteries."

"You'll have to wait and see."

"At least let me set up a meeting with a publisher. Let me make it up to you by doing this."

"You really liked it," Kevin said once again.

"Yes, I really liked it. Let's celebrate, wine and a quiet dinner at home, just the two of us," she said pulling him toward her and kissing him.

She liked it, Kevin thought.

Hold fast to dreams
for if dreams die
Life is a broken winged bird
that cannot fly.
Langston Hughes

VII

"I've got some time off coming. I would love to see you again. How about I come see you in two weeks?" That message had come two weeks ago. Kate had reluctantly said yes, then regretted it.

"Too late. I've already made my flight arrangements. Would you meet me at the local airport?"

"They don't fly passenger flights anymore."

"Don't worry about that. It's all taken care of." Don't worry, he says. Easy for him to say. Her life was out of control. First Terri gone, then this stranger from her past flies back into her life. And what about Tom? What should she tell Tom? Frank knew about Tom. It came up when he had asked her if she were seeing anyone. What was wrong with two old friends getting together to talk over old times? Certainly there was nothing wrong with that. Frank didn't think so, and neither did Tom when she told him.

"Of course you should see him. He's an old friend."

"An old boyfriend," Kate corrected. She was a little concerned over his lack of concern.

"Look, you'll regret it if you don't see him." Kate realized that was true. "And then you'd resent me for keeping you from seeing him."

"Possibly," Kate agreed.

"Hey, we're not kids, you and I. If what we have is meant to be, it'll take more than an old boyfriend, or an old girlfriend for that matter, to tear us apart."

"What do you mean, old girlfriend? Are you planning on looking up an old flame?"

"No, that's not what I mean . . ."

"It better not be."

"I just mean that we're not exclusive. You're free to go out with other men. I'm free to go out with other women . . ."

"Are you?"

"Am I what?"

"Going out with other women?"

"No, of course not. Why are you making this so difficult?"

"I'm sorry. I don't know why."

"If you are looking for an excuse to not see him, you'll have to look elsewhere. What are you afraid of? Don't you want to see him again? Even if we were exclusive, even if we were married, I'd still want you to see him if that was what you wanted. What is the problem?"

"I don't know," Kate admitted. Why did Tom have to be so damn reasonable, she thought? So here she was on a beautiful fall Friday afternoon, waiting for this stranger to fly back into her life.

She wasn't sure what to look for. He had said to meet him at three o'clock. She had managed to leave work early and made sure she would not be on call this weekend. The airport lobby was small and empty. The only business was the local car rental. They had stopped flying passenger flights about ten years ago. Now it was used for private airplanes and some commercial shipping. The local community college also had a flight school located at the airport. She had wondered before where they would find enough people in this city with both the interest and the money to take flying lessons, but apparently there was enough to keep the school open.

She often drove past the airport on her way to the shelter but had rarely stopped. One time, when Terri had been little, they had seen a convoy of helicopters landing at the airport and had stopped to watch them, grabbing a snack at the airport restaurant. The only other time she had stopped had been the time her car had broken down and she had to get a rental car.

Kate walked out to the viewing area, unsure what to look for. There was one small airplane from the flight school preparing for take-off, and another coming in. She leaned on the fence and watched.

"Kate?" Kate jumped as a forgotten, yet familiar voice spoke her name. She turned around to see an older face than she remembered but definitely Frank's face.

"I'm sorry. I didn't mean to startle you."

"How did you know it was me?"

"I'd have known you anywhere, Katy. I could never forget your face."

Kate smiled self-consciously. "When did you get here? And how?"

"I've got my ways. I haven't been a pilot all of my life without making a few connections. I got here earlier than I had expected. I was just hanging out with some of the flight instructors. You want to go for a ride?"

"Whoa. I haven't seen you in thirty years and now I'm supposed to jump into one of those tiny little airplanes with you?"

"Come on, it'll be fun. Don't you trust me?"

"No, I don't. Should I?"

"Maybe not," Frank said with a smile. "Gosh, it's good to see you. I've got reservations at the local Comfort Inn. How about you show me how to get there so I can check in, get settled and then we can get something to eat?"

"Sounds like a plan."

Kate insisted on driving him around the town. At first he had resisted, wanting to rent a car and drive himself.

"What's the matter, don't you trust me?" she asked him.

"Should I?"

"I haven't killed anybody yet. Come on."

"There's always a first time," Frank said as he climbed in. "I guess I'm too used to being in the driver's seat."

"Then maybe it's time you learned." The grand tour took all of an hour. Kate felt better being behind the wheel of her car, more in control of the situation. "Where would you like to eat?" she asked.

"It's your town. Surprise me," Frank responded.

"How about Italian?"

"Anything," Frank agreed. Kate didn't want to take him to the deli where she and Tom had had their first date. Besides, it was getting a little cold for eating outside. The Italian restaurant had been one of Terri's favorites and wasn't far from the Comfort Inn where Frank was staying. It seemed like a good neutral setting and hopefully wouldn't be too crowded with teenagers because of the football game tonight.

"I used to come here a lot with my daughter," Kate commented as they were seated.

"Yes, Terri. Wish I could meet her. Have you heard anything recently?"

"Not too much. You know, I'm just her mom. She saves all the good stuff for her friends. How's Chad?"

"Good. He's still in the states, much to his mother's relief and my relief."

"It's hard, isn't it? Being in the military. Having your son in the military."

"It's all I ever knew. Even those years when I was flying commercial flights. I thought I wanted out, couldn't wait to be a civilian but then . . . I don't know. I guess it's in my blood. Still it's not easy. What about you? Is it hard being a, what is it you do? A social worker? All those sad stories you have to hear, dysfunctional families you have to make functional."

"It is hard sometimes, but I always wanted to help others. So that's why I went into social work. I guess I'm just a bleeding-heart liberal."

"Or just a good person who cares. I always knew that about you, Katy. You were just a good, kind person who wanted to help. That's what attracted me to you in the first place."

Kate stared down in embarrassment at the pasta that had been placed in front of her. She was glad for an excuse to not respond.

Frank paused as he took a sip of wine then asked, "So what happened to us?"

"What do you mean, what happened to us? You know what happened. You had to go to school a thousand miles away. You didn't write. We lost contact with each other. It happens all the time."

"Maybe, but did you ever wonder what might have been? What if things had been different? I know I've wondered."

"Frank, we hardly knew each other. We still don't really know each other. Why spend a lot of time wondering about what might have been?"

"I guess when you're in the cockpit flying hours on end, you have a lot of time to wonder about what might have been. But, you know, you're right. We really didn't know each other back then and don't know each other now, so here's to getting to know each other," Frank raised his glass in a toast.

"That I can drink to," Kate smiled as they clicked glasses.

Kate dropped Frank off at the entrance to the Comfort Inn after dinner.

"Do you want to meet for breakfast?" Frank asked. "I hear they have a good special at the airport restaurant. I could meet you there."

"How about ten a.m.?" Kate suggested. Friends, just friends, she told herself. For some reason she didn't want him showing up at her home just yet. She wanted to take this slow. You can't cram thirty years into one weekend. Besides, there was still Tom to consider. It was still early when she got home. She went to bed and tossed and turned through most of the night.

"You know this was a ruse," Frank said after breakfast the next day.

"What was?"

"Getting you to meet me at the airport. It was just a ruse to get you into an airplane with me," Frank told her.

"Then it wasn't all that well thought out. You don't really want to take me up in a small plane after a breakfast of pancakes, eggs and bacon, do you?"

"You'll be fine," Frank insisted.

"And if I'm not, you promise you'll take me down." Rushing back into her memory came the ride on the Octopus at the fair thirty years ago, her clinging to Frank's arm for dear life, her stomach churning and face green.

"I promise. I've got a great day planned for us. Just trust me. If you don't trust me, then trust the airplane."

Now that's comforting, Kate thought as she climbed into the seat behind the pilot.

"Remember the Octopus," she reminded Frank.

"Yeah," Frank said with a smile. "I didn't know a face could be such a combination of pale and green. I thought you were going to pull my arm out of the socket. Don't worry, this will be much better. I promise."

Kate wasn't sure why or how she finally made it into the plane but with confidence she didn't know she had, she pushed past her fear in order to give it a try. Before she knew it they were in the air, soaring over the tops of trees.

"I had a buddy plot the course for us," Frank commented over the roar of the engine.

"How many buddies do you have? I didn't know you knew anyone from here."

"Well . . ." Frank began.

"I know, you have a lot of connections."

Frank smiled, "He said this would be a great route to take to see the fall color."

Kate pushed her heart back down into her chest and looked at the familiar sight of her city, seen from a whole new perspective. Then they were beyond the city and farms and trees spread out below them. The trees were ablaze with fall color. They seemed to be floating above them, even with the roar of the engines.

"Bet you've never seen the trees quite like this," Frank said.

"This is great," Kate shouted.

"I'll come in closer." They flew over the tops of the trees then circled around. Kate settled in her seat trying to take in every bit of the view.

"You up for some stunt flying?" Frank asked.

"What?!"

"Just watch," Frank said as he pulled across a cornfield, swooped low then circled up. "You okay?"

"Yes," Kate said, grasping her seat, "no loop-de-loops, please."

Frank smiled as he set a course for some hills in the distance. Kate sat back and enjoyed the ride.

"Want to try your hand at this?" Frank asked.

"Oh no, I'm quite fine just sitting here."

"Okay then. Guess it's time to head back."

Kate watched as the familiar sight of the city reappeared.

"That was incredible," she said as she wobbled down from the plane, almost falling on Frank.

"You liked it? You looked a little unsure at times."

"Well, yeah, like when we hit those air pockets, but it was great."

"You know how they say there are no atheists in foxholes. I don't see how there can be atheists in the sky. You look out at that great immense sky, you touch the clouds with your wings and you just know, there's got to be something, someone greater out there. It truly is like touching the face of God."

"You love flying, don't you?"

"It's my life, that and the military."

"What about the missions you flew in the Middle East?"

"That was different. That was when you prayed that God would get you through, and God did. Those weren't good times. You flew blind, relying on your instrument panel to keep you safe, help you find the target. Those aren't the times I prefer to remember."

"But God got you through," Kate said softly and took his hand.

"Yes, God has got me through so far," Frank said seriously, looking off into space, seemingly unaware of her presence. "You know, there's a lot of trust involved in flying. You have to trust your mechanics to keep your plane in good condition; you have to trust the controls. When you are in the air, it's just you and the machine, any mechanical problems and our lives would be in grave danger, and yet we pilots keep flying. Guess you have to be a little crazy."

"And you have to love it."

"That I do." They walked hand in hand from the plane back to their cars.

"How about I drive this time?"

"But you don't know where to go . . ."

"Hey," Frank interrupted her.

"All right, I know, you've got connections," Kate said with a laugh. "I guess if I can get into a plane with you, I can ride in a car with you."

The rest of the day flew by before they knew it. They walked in the park together, sat together on a bench watching the ducks, their coats wrapped around them. They ate at a quiet restaurant before Frank drove her back to the airport to pick up her car.

Frank backed his car into the spot next to her car. "Remember our first kiss?"

"How could I forget? You were trying to put the move on me all night with no success. I was beginning to think you really didn't want to kiss me."

"No, that wasn't the case. I just wanted the best time to make my move."

"You certainly took your time."

"Remember how I backed into your driveway."

"Then you got me to look back at my house," Kate said as they both looked to the back of the car.

"Then I leaned over . . ." Frank leaned over.

". . . and kissed me," Kate said as they kissed softly.

They pulled away. "Then I said good night, went into my home, into my room, shut the door and said, wow, my first kiss," Kate said.

"Your first kiss."

"Yes, my first kiss. You never forget your first kiss, regardless of where your life takes you. I've never forgotten you."

"Nor I you . . ." They stared into each other's eyes for a few seconds then Kate said, "I guess I better be going."

"Be that way."

"What? What do you mean by that? That's what you used to say. I never knew what you were referring to. It used to bug me."

"Just a phrase I used to get to you."

"Well, it did. Guess I better go."

"Guess you better go," he agreed but neither moved.

"Be that way," Kate said as she turned to open the door. Frank reached over and pulled her back to him as they kissed repeatedly.

"Now I really have to go. When do you leave tomorrow?"

"Noon."

"Do you want to meet for breakfast?"

"We don't have to meet."

"What do you mean?"

"We don't have to meet for breakfast if we never leave."

"You mean spend the night?"

"It's a possibility."

"Can't do that. You waltz back into my life after thirty years. We spend one day together and you expect us to end up in bed. I can't do that. I don't do that."

"Just a suggestion. I'm sorry."

"So am I," Kate said as she opened the door.

"Hey, I still want to have breakfast with you. Will I see you before I leave?"

"I don't know," Kate said as she drove away.

Damn, Frank thought. That did not go the way he had intended. Not the sleeping part. He had never intended that they would spend the night together. It just came out. It felt so good being together. And now it was over. Frank went back to his room and stared at the phone. Would she be home yet? He wondered. Finally he picked up the phone and called.

Kate jumped when the phone rang even though she had been expecting it. This was not how she had wanted the evening to end.

"Hello."

"I'm sorry. I didn't mean for the evening to end like this. I don't know why I said what I did. It just came out. It's just, I was having such a good time with you, I didn't want the evening to end. Do you forgive me?" Frank paused and waited for her response.

Kate paused before saying, "I'm sorry too. I shouldn't have got so upset. It's not like we're kids anymore. It's just, I'm not like that. No matter how much I like a guy, I'm just not like that."

"I know you're not. I was just stupid. Can we have breakfast tomorrow? I don't want to leave without seeing you again."

"I don't know. What good will it do? I mean, you have to go back to your life and I have mine. It was great seeing you . . . I just don't know. I'll think about it." Kate hung up, went to bed, but didn't sleep. Her mind was racing. What would it hurt, seeing him again? After all, he came all this way to see her. The least she could do was say goodbye. But then what? A long distance romance? That was not for her. Why couldn't they just be friends? They're just friends. She would just go to the airport to say goodbye and they would just be friends, she assured herself and finally went to sleep.

Frank arrived at the airport early in the hopes she would be there. He smiled with relief when he saw her arrive.

"I'm so glad you came. I didn't want to leave without saying goodbye."

"And I didn't want you to leave without saying goodbye. I had a good time yesterday."

"We aren't saying goodbye for forever."

"Aren't we? When will we see each other again?"

"Is that the problem? I can come again."

"But your work. Remember, you're married to the military."

"I get time off for good behavior. Look, we will see each other again. I can't go another thirty years without you in my life."

"Don't say things you don't truly mean. It was good seeing you. I had a good time yesterday. That's enough for today. Goodbye, Frank."

"I'll be back. I'll show you. I will be back. I've got to go, but I'll be back," Frank said as he turned to board his plane.

"Goodbye," Kate said as she watched his plane depart.

Kate jumped when the phone rang. She had been expecting it to ring all day and yet now that it had she jumped as if surprised.

"How was your weekend?" Tom's voice sounded on the other end.

"It was all right, good, actually, good."

"You want to go out for a drink and talk?"

"No, not tonight. I'm really tired. Another time."

"Lunch tomorrow?"

"Sure. Sounds good." She didn't want to lose a great guy like Tom for some fantasy flyboy, but she also wasn't ready to talk to anyone. When she checked her email there was a message from Frank.

He doesn't waste any time, she thought. He must have written this the minute he got home. Correction, on the way home. The message had been sent while still in flight.

"Katy, I had a great weekend. It was so good to see you. I will see you again. I will gain your trust again, I promise. Just give me a chance. Frank"

Give him a chance? Give him a chance? What did he call this weekend? It was . . . nice, very nice. Why did this have to happen? Why did he have to come back into her life, now when she had a great guy she was dating? Someone she cared for and trusted. Why did he have to show up to disturb her life? She didn't trust him, as much as she cared for him. And even if she trusted him, what was she to do? Quit her job, move to wherever he was stationed and then worry about him whenever he went to fight? It was no life for her.

86

Still it was nice to see him. She felt younger. All of the years just melted away while they were together. But Tom, Tom was real, not some fantasy from her teen years. He was real, kind, stable. He cared for her, or so she thought. Did he? Or was she just convenient? Frank certainly inconvenienced himself for her. What was she thinking? She was much too old for this.

She had to focus on her work. If only her sister weren't so busy with that election. She could have talked to her. Helen could have helped her figure this out. She was so level-headed. But no, she was too busy to be bothered now.

No email from Terri. If only Terri were here. Then I'd be too busy for all of this dating, too busy for men, she thought. I miss Terri.

What was I doing, Frank thought even as he sent Kate the email. Maybe she was right. He was married to the military. His life wasn't his own, especially not right now, not with everything happening in the Middle East. And yet that's part of why he just had to see her. He knew he didn't have time for a relationship and yet he couldn't stand the thought of never seeing her again. And yet I may not see her, he thought. Was I wrong telling her I would, promising things I had no right to promise? I will see her again, he vowed. I just had to. It had been hard getting away for the weekend, but he had done it. He could do it again. She is not a security risk. He didn't tell her anything and yet is that fair to her either, to keep her in the dark? Yet national security relied on it.

I have to see her again. I have to give this a real chance. Not like before. I can't lose her again. Not yet anyway. Not until we've really had a chance. We didn't have a chance thirty years ago. We deserve a chance now, he told himself.

"Don," she stopped her husband from getting out of the car. He looked over at her. "You know I'm not going to win."

"Don't say that yet. You never know what might happen."

"No, we both know. No sense in pretending. I just wanted to say it now, before I have to go in and put on a false face, pretend we have a chance when I know we don't. And I wanted to thank you so much for your help and support. I don't know what I would have done without you." She hushed him as she saw him preparing to speak. "I just wanted a chance and I got it. I wanted to see if I could do it, wanted to try to make a difference, do something more. Thank you for supporting me in this. I know it wasn't what you had planned on doing in your retirement. When it's over we will take that trip, do what you want. After all, you worked hard for so many years to support me and the kids. And now this. It's the least I can do for you. Thank you." She leaned over and kissed him.

"Are you forgetting you have an election to win, Ms. State Representative?" Don teased.

"Okay, I'm ready now," she said and climbed out of the car.

She lost, as expected; but the margin was much smaller than anyone had expected, forty-four percent to fifty-three percent. For a relative unknown! She graciously ceded to her rival, who called her a worthy adversary and campaigner. She fell exhausted into bed that night and slept past noon.

"So what do we do now?" she asked Don when he surprised her with breakfast in bed. "No phone calls to return, no meetings to run to, no rallies or press conferences, what shall I do with myself?"

"Whatever you want. You're still on sabbatical, you know. And actually, you do have a phone call to return. It seems the leaders of the party were so impressed by your run that they want to groom you for another position. What do you think of that?"

"I think I'm still on sabbatical. I think I want to rest for a while. And I think we have a vacation to plan," she told him with a kiss.

Dover Beach, Matthew Arnold

VIII

"So are you?"

"Am I what?"

"Going to see him again?"

"I don't know," she had answered honestly. She just didn't know. So many things she didn't know. But how could she tell Tom that? He was a friend, and yet more than a friend. How could she tell him how confused she was? Would I see him again, she asked herself. Despite Frank's promises she couldn't believe it. He would email for several days in a row and then there would be those long gaps in between, weeks at a time. It was almost as if that October weekend had never happened. She hadn't known what to tell Tom then and still didn't know what to say now.

She was so confused. It was as if the bottom had fallen out of her life when Terri had left leaving this huge hole into which Frank had appeared. She didn't understand it. It wasn't as if it was the end of the world. Kids grow up; they leave home. In some ways it was a relief not to have her around to worry about, although worry she still did, just a different fashion of worry. All of a sudden she had all this free time, but she didn't know what to do with it. Tom certainly had his ideas, but they weren't hers. She wanted her ideas, her own dreams to fulfill.

Somewhere along the line of her life she had lost her dreams. She knew she had had them, once upon a time, but now they were gone. Gone amidst a divorce and just growing up. The disillusionment of growing old, realizing she wasn't going to accomplish the myriad of things she had dreamed about as a girl.

When did her dreams shift from her own to her child? Dreams for this child and her future. She knew the craziness of that. Terri needed her own dreams, not ones imposed from her mother. She knew it was crazy to put all your dreams for a future on your children, and in her case, just one child. Poor Terri. No wonder she had needed to leave. Had I been suffocating her without realizing it, she wondered. Sure, I gave her a lot of freedom, but having to live with my unspoken dreams, too much for anyone.

"What happened?" she asked Helen over lunch.

"I lost, no big deal. It was fun just to be in the running."

"No, I mean what happened to our dreams? We were going to do something great. Both of us. We both wanted something more, didn't we? I was going to change the world, maybe work for the United Nations. Do something for world peace. So much for all of those years of studying French."

"You are making the world better one person at a time."

"I know, and so are you, but are we really? How much are we really accomplishing, how much have we done? And now, here I am, getting closer and closer to fifty and what have I done?"

"You've got Terri."

"No, that's the worst of it. Somehow over the years, despite my determination not to do this, despite all my studies in counseling and the women I have counseled not to do this, I find I've placed all my hopes and dreams for my future on my child. It's so wrong of me."

"Sounds pretty human to me."

"Did you do this with your daughters?"

"Oh, hard to remember, those teen years seem so long ago. I guess if I did, those dreams were quickly shattered by reality and my daughters' independent streak. No way they were going to let me put my dreams on them. One thing I did do, that was to raise strong, independent daughters."

"That Terri is as well."

"Sometimes I wonder if I did too good a job. Would be nice if they needed me now and then," Helen smiled. "Now my dream is for grandchildren, if my daughters would just get married."

"I'm not ready for that."

"You will be. So tell me, how's your love life?"

Kate filled her in. "Wow, I have been out of the loop for a while. Two men. Now that the election is over, I expect you to give me every detail. How else will I be able to live vicariously through you?"

"How are things between you and Don now that he's retired?"

"Better than I ever imagined it could be, better than I could have dreamed. Who would have thought that one day I would wake up and find myself back in love with him, more than when we first got married, better than when we married because of all the years. Sometimes dreams do come true."

"I'm so happy for you, Helen. Glad to know that some people's dreams, even ones they didn't know they had, do come true."

Kate reflected on her conversation with her sister. It wasn't an overnight switch, the switch to dreaming for her daughter. It had happened gradually, over time. In some ways it was the natural outcome of trying to be a good mother, putting your child first, denying yourself for her. After so many years of putting Terri first, putting her own dreams on hold, it just seemed natural to dream dreams for her daughter, no matter how hard she tried to avoid this. She had put her own dreams on hold for so long that she had none left for herself. What good was a life without a dream? What were some of her dreams from her childhood? Did she ever have dreams of her own?

There had been a time when she had wanted to do something for world peace. Certainly that was a worthwhile goal. That had been part of the motivating force behind her involvement in the peace movement where she had met Terri's dad. Then she had decided she would try to make this a better world one person at a time and went into social work. But after six years at the shelter, she felt she was seeing too many revolving doors, teens repeating the cycle of poverty and abuse as adults and too few success stories. She wondered, was it really worth it? Was she really making an impact?

All of this had been below the surface for years, waiting for the right event or chain of events to bring it to the top. Terri's leaving had been that event. Her house, newly transformed, symbolized the waste of her life. All of that work to no avail, for no reason. Sure it hadn't been a complete waste, but it hadn't been the best use of resources. Time was running out. She was far from young and while retirement was still years away, she felt the passage of time, ever speeding up, creeping up on her until it would be too late for her, too late to make any changes and here she would be trapped in this house, in this town, in her job. Terri certainly didn't let concern for her mother keep her from trying something new. Maybe it was time for her to try something new as well.

Into this sudden void came this memory from her past. But not just a memory. A real flesh-and-blood person. Sure, she hadn't known Tom for long, hadn't really given the relationship a chance, but somehow he was the one connected to her past in Kate's mind, not Frank. He was the one holding her back to this house, this town. Frank wasn't just a shadow from her past but an invitation for a future. A whole new future where people get second chances, second chances for love and for life.

What was she thinking, practical Kate? Was she actually contemplating chucking it all, starting out somewhere new with someone new and yet not new? Or was it just the siren song of change, the desire to do something, anything, just so she didn't have to stay in this emptiness that was her house, her life? Why did she feel like her whole life was over, then along came Frank to throw her a rescue line, a love line, a love lost and then found? Or was this just the wild machinations of mid-life crisis exacerbated by empty nest syndrome? She didn't care. She just wanted the emptiness to go away.

It was increasingly hard to keep up appearances at work. She still showed up, put in her time, but something was missing from her work, a certain spark. It was starting to affect the quality of her work. Her boss had tried to talk to her about it, but Kate kept putting her off.

"It's nothing. I'm okay, just a little tired maybe, and, of course, I miss Terri, but she's going to be home for two weeks at Christmas. I'm planning on taking time off then, if I can get your okay. The time will do me good."

"I hope so. I'm worried about you, Kate."

"Nothing to worry about, Diane. I'm fine," Kate said but inside she knew she was lying, still how she could she talk to

Diane any more than she could talk to Tom? If she told Diane what was going through her head she might be without a job. She had to hang onto her job until she knew what she wanted to do.

The emails from Frank were only slightly more frequent and informative than the ones from Terri. That just seemed to make her wonder all the more. He was hiding something, something he couldn't tell her. But then, it couldn't be that difficult to guess with all the talk of war in the Middle East. There was no question in Kate's mind that Frank was somehow involved with planning any air strike that might be part of a military initiative in Iraq. So why all the secrecy?

Still she understood and didn't press Frank for details about his work. She was more interested in whether he would be getting away any time soon to visit, but that didn't seem to be in the offing. She both wanted to see him again and dreaded it. To have him here, in the flesh, made everything too real. It was so much nicer to fantasize. You didn't have to deal with messy reality that way. He could be her dream lover waiting to sweep her off her feet, take her away from all of this. Together they could ride off into the sunset. Yes, there was something to be said about a dream lover. No strings attached, or actually, the strings were hers to pull to make him act in any way she wanted. So different from flesh and blood relationships; easier than dealing with Tom.

At least she had Terri's visit to help keep her mind off of Frank, and Tom for that matter. She had hardly said good-bye and put away the Christmas stuff when she received an email from Frank.

"I have to see you. I was able to arrange to get away next weekend. This may be my last opportunity for a long while. Please say you'll meet me at the airport this Friday at 3 p.m."

Frank knew he was getting himself in deeper with this relationship but he wasn't getting any younger. Sure, maybe he should wait till things cool down in the Middle East, wait until he really could offer her something, but what if things didn't cool down for a long time, years? How long was he to put his life on hold for the military? How much did he owe the military? Hadn't he given enough? Didn't he deserve this chance for love? But then what of her? Was it fair to her? Regardless, he had to see her again. If he didn't see her then, who knows when he would see her? Plans for war were progressing, could be as early as February or March. He had to take the time while he could.

Kate waited with anticipation for his flight to get in. Fortunately the weather had cooperated and he had clear, if cold, skies for flying. Her heart jumped in her chest as she saw him walk down the steps and across the runway. She awkwardly stretched out her hand in welcome. He took her hand, smiled and said, "It's great to see you." They both seemed uncertain what to say or do next.

"Let's get inside where it's warmer," Kate suggested.

"Good idea," Frank responded as they both were slightly shivering from the cold.

"I thought we'd have dinner at my place," Kate said once they got into the warmth of the terminal. "It will be easier to talk there."

"Whatever you say. Just let me get settled in at the motel then I'll be all yours." Frank started to arrange for a rental car when Kate intervened.

"You know, you can use my car. I don't have anything that I absolutely have to have a car for. Fortunately I'm not on call this weekend." Kate had been surprised at how easy it had been to switch her weekend on call. She had expected trouble after just having two weeks off but Diane had been amenable.

"You know, I have a perfectly good spare room that's not being used. You're welcome to stay there," Kate suggested.

"Are you sure?"

"Sure, I can trust you, can't I?"

Frank smiled and said, "We'll see about that."

"Besides, the house won't seem so empty with someone in Terri's room." Kate felt suddenly unsure about what she was doing. It had seemed so logical when she had planned it. It wasn't an invitation to sleep together, just a chance to have more time together. Now she wasn't so sure about the suggestion.

Frank must have seen the hesitation in her eyes.

"You know, it's okay. It's probably better if I have my own space. I wouldn't want to inconvenience you."

"It's not an inconvenience," Kate assured him none too convincingly.

"If you're sure," Frank agreed. The drive to Kate's was awkward. Frank seemed different, older, more tired, than the other time. He wasn't so much the teenage boy she remembered but a man with a man's burdens. She wondered if she was making a mistake, having him stay at her home. What would Tom say, not that it was any of his business. They weren't exclusive. Still if she wasn't doing anything wrong, why this need for silence?

It was all too confusing. Soon though, Frank would be gone again and just a memory that she could pack neatly away into the recesses of her mind. A memory she could dust off now and then, but a memory none-the-less. Didn't she deserve a few good memories? And if the weekend became more than the meeting of two old friends, didn't she deserve that, too? Didn't she deserve a fling now and then? But this wasn't to be a fling.

"How was your flight?" she asked.

"Uneventful, a little bumpy, but worth every bump in that it was bringing me to you."

Kate smiled. That sounded more like the old Frank. Always the flirt. She pulled into her driveway and parked. Frank carried his suitcase and briefcase.

"Work?" Kate asked him.

"My computer. I have to check in, stay on top of any new happenings. Hope you don't mind."

"No," Kate said as she showed him into the house. Cookie came running up to check Frank out.

"Hey, girl," Frank put down his luggage and leaned over and petted her. "Do I meet your approval?"

"We'll see," Kate said. "It may be easy to snow Cookie, but I'm not as much of a pushover. Terri's room is upstairs if you want to take your things up there."

"Wait," Frank said, "how about a proper hello." He reached over, pulled her into his arms and kissed her. "It's so good to see you, Katie."

Kate leaned into the embrace. "It's good to see you, too." She offered no resistance to his kiss. "Now why don't you put your stuff away?" Frank went upstairs while she went into the kitchen.

"Would you like some coffee?" she called upstairs to him.

"Sounds great," his words echoed down the stairs. It seemed so nice to have a man in the house. Tom had come over for dinner a couple of times and watched a video with her, but this was different. "I'm going to take a quick shower then I'll be right down."

Kate started the coffee. The smell drifted through the kitchen and upstairs. She poured herself a cup and sat down at the breakfast nook with the afternoon paper.

"Smells good," Frank came into the room barefoot in jeans and a sweatshirt. His hair was still damp, although neatly combed. Kate jumped up to get him a cup.

"You don't have to wait on me, Katy. In fact, the least I can do is take you out to eat at some place nice tonight. Any place you want."

"That would be great," Kate responded, suddenly feeling very shy. It seems she had imagined this so many times in her dreams, but now it was happening.

The evening passed all too quickly – dinner and dancing. The time flew by and the years seemed to fade as they were transported to another time and place when both of them had been so much younger. It was hard to say good-bye, even though their rooms were just across the hall from each other. Or perhaps this was what made it harder. The awareness of the presence of Frank just a short distance away weighed heavily in Kate's mind. Her body, too long without the presence of a man, craved him next to her. And yet she knew it was wrong and so resisted.

She was up early, drinking coffee, reading the paper and staring into space.

"Smells good," Frank startled her coming in once again with bare feet, wearing jeans and a sweatshirt. His hair was still wet from his shower.

"Did you sleep all right?"

"Great, and you?"

"Great," she lied. She couldn't tell him she tossed and turned all night. "Are you hungry?"

"Ravenous." They lingered over breakfast, talking about what they would do for the rest of the day.

"How about I cook for you?" Frank suggested.

"Oh, no, you're my guest."

"I want to. I don't get to cook for others too often. I see the grill on your deck. I could grill us some steaks. How does that sound?"

96

"Sounds good to me, if you're willing to shovel a path to the grill."

"No problem."

Kate had to go into the office for a short while that afternoon. She was still trying to get caught up after two weeks of vacation. Frank stayed at her house and got caught up with some of his work. When she came back they went grocery shopping for their dinner.

As they sat down over a bottle of red wine, steaks, salad and baked potatoes, Frank grew silent. The tired look she had seen in the car reappeared.

"Tired?" she asked and reached across the table to take his hand.

"No, just thinking."

"What about?"

"Nothing that concerns you."

"Try me." Frank had grown so serious. She had remembered this side of him from thirty years ago as well. A sadder side.

"Thinking about how quickly the weekend is passing."

"Too quickly," Kate agreed.

"And what I have to go back to."

"More problems in the Middle East?"

"More problems. I don't want to go there, don't want to think about it tonight. Tomorrow will be here soon enough."

"You don't have to pretend with me. It's pretty obvious we are on the verge of war. Everyone knows that."

"Yes, well everyone knows, but they don't know. They don't know the half of it," he paused, "Let's talk of better things like when will I see you again?"

"It's up to you."

"Do you think you could get away for a weekend if I can arrange a flight for you?"

"I don't know. I guess it depends on the weekend. You mean visit you in Washington?"

"Sure. It would be great. There's so much to do. It would be good to see you."

After dinner they sat before the fire and talked and sat in silence until they finally agreed it was time to go upstairs. Once again they walked up the stairs together, said good night and prepared to go to their separate rooms.

Now or never, Kate thought as they kissed good-bye. But now that the moment seemed right, it was impossible. She couldn't do it. She didn't know why something kept her from inviting him into her room. She shut her door then stood beside the door for several minutes trying to decide what to do. Why hadn't she acted on those moments when she had felt such a desire? Why couldn't she be swept away by the moment? That would have been her excuse. She had been swept away. No decision made, just giving into feeling. Why did she have to make a decision? Why? And why was it so hard to make?

Slowly she opened the door to her room. The light was still on in Frank's room. Should she? Dare she? She knocked softly on the door. No answer. She was about to go back into her room when the door opened.

Frank stepped out in his bathrobe, "Is something wrong?"

"No, yes, no, fine, everything's fine, goodnight."

"Goodnight then."

"No, it's not all right. It won't be all right. Terri's gone and tomorrow you'll be gone and, I want to have tonight," Kate said softly.

"I want that too," Frank said as he took her into his arms and softly kissed her lips. Kate took him by the hand and led him into her room.

"Remember the time I tried to seduce you?"

"Of course. Luring an innocent young girl to an empty house. Why didn't you?"

"Don't know. Just didn't seem right. You were so naïve. It felt like taking advantage of you. I didn't want to do that."

"Instead you waited thirty years for me to take advantage of you. Was it worth the wait?"

"I don't know. Let's try it again," Frank leaned over and kissed her.

Kate laughed, "And what about breakfast?"

"Who needs breakfast? Not me. I'm a soldier. I can exist on K-rations. Just give me some loving."

"Well, I can't, exist on K-rations," Kate began to get out of bed.

"One more time, for old time sake."

"I've heard that line before," Kate laughed as he pulled her back.

"And I've used it before. Never worked though."

"Until today." Kate allowed herself to be enfolded in his arms.

"Until today," he repeated with a smile and kiss.

The morning went by far too quickly for both of them. Long before they were ready it was time to leave. Kate drove Frank to the airport. She accompanied him to the door to the runway. They had already said their goodbyes, over and over that morning. Frank hugged her to him in a deep embrace.

"No tears," he said. "Remember, I'll see you again."

"No tears," Kate said with a forced smile. "Till we meet again."

She watched as he walked across to the plane. She waved as he got on and again when the plane took off then left. She didn't want to stay there any longer than necessary. The airport lobby seemed cold and unfriendly, taking away her friend. There was nothing left to do but go back to her cold car and drive to her empty house, all alone, once again all alone.

Their cruise was scheduled to begin right after Christmas. Helen and Don spent Christmas with their children then took a flight to the Florida Keys where they embarked aboard their luxury cruise liner the next day. It was to be a second honeymoon plus a celebration of his retirement, her sabbatical and her lost election.

"Just think," she said as they strolled on deck the first night and gazed at the moonlight. "If I had been elected I'd be busy right now preparing to set up my office. I think I got the better end of the deal, don't you?"

Don picked up two glasses of champagne from a waiter walking by and handed her one.

"Here's to losing the election. The best thing that could have happened to us."

"Not the best thing, but maybe the second best. The best was finding each other again."

"I'll drink to that."

They spent the next morning snorkeling in exotic coves. Then, after lunch in an outdoor café, they walked hand in hand through the markets at their first port of call. By dusk Don wasn't quite feeling like himself.

"Too much tropical sun," he said as he sent Helen to dinner without him.

"Are you sure you're okay? We can have dinner in our cabin?"

"I'm fine. I just don't feel like eating. You go ahead and enjoy yourself."

Despite what Don had said, it was difficult for Helen to enjoy herself. She ate a light dinner, picking at the food on her plate, anxious to get back to check on Don. She brought some food back with her to their cabin, opened the door and called his name but he did not respond. She found him on the floor of the bathroom.

IX

It wasn't as bad as she had thought it would be. The days went by quickly. She saw Josh now and then. He'd smile and wave. She smiled back. "I am so over him," she told herself each time. It was only when she came home for Christmas that it hit her how much she missed home. She had been surprised when her mom hadn't immediately agreed to her moving back. What was going on here? And what was the deal with these men? Tom and that other one she hadn't met! Did her mom actually have a life of her own? Seemed too ridiculous for Terri to even consider. Still Mom had seemed almost anxious for her to leave. She had wanted her to at least finish out the semester and then she had said she could talk about coming home.

"Did you have a good Christmas?" her dad asked as they drove from the airport. This time he had come alone. The novelty of having a big sister around had long ago worn off, so her stepmom had stayed home with Alex and Alyssa. It was nice, this time together.

"Yeah, it was good. Mom says hi."

"How is she doing without you?"

"Actually, I think she's dating."

"Good for her. It's about time."

"I guess."

"What's wrong?"

"It's just so weird, Mom dating after all these years."

"And why shouldn't she date? I'm surprised no one has come along before this."

"It's weird and it's even weirder talking to you about it."

"Okay, enough said, but I'm glad for her. It's about time she started to do a few things for herself."

"Daddy!" she exclaimed when he continued to talk. He laughed and turned on the radio.

Terri thought about going home at semester break, but then she wouldn't have been able to finish what she had started with yearbook. She knew it would be too late to work on the yearbook at home. She missed her friends, but they all seemed to be doing just fine without her. That world hadn't ended when she left. The same dramas continued to be played out. Breakups and romance and gossip. She had caught up on it all over Christmas break, but then, after that, there had been little else to talk about.

Her friends talked about what was going on at her old school and what they were doing. They talked about the upcoming musical and of course the prom, but she wasn't part of that. It had felt weird. In some ways it was all so familiar, nothing had changed. In other ways everything was different. She wasn't really a part of their world right now. She knew she could return and rejoin her old friends, but it would have been hard coming back halfway through the year. She had a different school play to talk about and different prom to look forward to, and different friends. It was as if nothing had changed but the names and faces. So she had decided to stay and finish off the school year.

She had been having fun taking pictures this year. It had given her an excuse to go to Josh's cross-country races. At home she probably would have auditioned for the musical, at least been part of the chorus, but here she decided it would be more fun to watch from a distance, from a photographer's viewpoint. It was a relief not to be involved in the agony of try-outs, the heartache and rejection when you didn't get the part you so desperately wanted, but which you couldn't let anyone know that you wanted; the false nonchalance and bravado even though your heart was breaking. Instead she would capture it on camera.

And the prom. She wouldn't agonize about getting the perfect date; she would go as the yearbook photographer. She had made a pact with Sheri. Neither of them would have dates. They would go together, but then Sean from yearbook asked Sheri and she said yes.

At first she felt betrayed, but then she reminded herself she would be gone next year while Sheri would still be here. Sure, if she went to the prom without a date everyone would know she was a loser, but that wouldn't matter for her because next year she would be gone. It wasn't really "her" prom anyway. It was freeing, knowing that this was a temporary situation. So what if she wasn't on the homecoming court? It wasn't even her school – so how could she call it home? So what if she didn't have a date for the prom? It wasn't her prom. And if she had left, she would have missed the track season and seeing Josh in those adorable running shorts. It was worth staying just for that.

Josh had been true to his word, they were still friends. He really was a great guy. They weren't exactly best friends, but he didn't avoid her. He smiled and waved, even when with his latest girlfriend. But they were friends. "SIGH," she wrote in her journal.

"So, I guess that's where it's at."

"We can still be friends," Kate said

"Yeah, sure, friends."

"I'm sorry." She was and yet she wasn't. Part of her screamed, don't let him go. He's the best thing to come along in her life for years. And yet the decision had been made the night she slept with Frank. She couldn't pretend it didn't happen, even if Tom didn't know. She knew. She cared too much about him to pretend, to lead him on in anyway.

"I guess you're going to see him again, then."

"I think so, whenever he can get some time off."

"If it doesn't work out . . ." Tom started.

"I know, I know."

"It's hard to compete with a fantasy. By him being so far away, it prolongs the fantasy. If he were here, maybe I'd have more of a chance."

"Maybe," Kate agreed, "but then you have your memories as well."

"Yeah, I guess," Tom admitted, but he didn't agree.

What did she mean by that? My wife's been gone for over ten years. I'm not hanging on to her memory, am I? Kate was the first woman he was really interested in, but was there something between them that kept them from getting closer? Someones? Laura and Frank? Perhaps Kate was right. It's hard to compete with a memory.

"Goodbye," Tom leaned over and kissed Kate's cheek. He let himself out the door while Kate resisted the urge to call after him.

What is wrong with me, she wondered. I made my choice. Why these second thoughts? Hadn't I given Tom a real chance?

Maybe there wasn't a chance, not once Frank came back into my life. But Frank … Frank seemed so far away, not just miles away.

True to his word, several weeks later she was in Washington D.C. after a cramped ride in an airplane shipping freight.

"Next time, I make the arrangements," Kate told Frank at the gate. He whisked her away for what was to be a fun-filled weekend in Washington but they hardly left his apartment. There was an intensity about Frank. He didn't say so, but Kate knew the problems in Iraq and possible war were never far from his thoughts. The phone rang several times over the weekend. Frank would check the number then say,

"Sorry, I have to take this." Then he would go into another room to talk.

"Next time you come see me so you can get away from work."

"Sure, sounds like a plan," Frank agreed, but Kate realized there wasn't likely to be a next time soon. Frank didn't have to say anything. He showed her around the Pentagon and introduced her to his son, but other than that, most of their time was spent in his apartment. They made love passionately and tenderly, holding on to each other as if it would be the last time.

It was fun and exciting to be away from everything familiar. She felt younger as if shedding years when with Frank. But it was also intense. She came home exhausted from the intensity of the weekend and more confused than ever. It was comforting to get back home, back to normalcy. It was comforting to read her email and get a cryptic message from Terri. Terri never wasted a word, it seemed. It was good to get home, yet she felt strangely alone, more alone than even before she had gone. She found herself missing Tom but assured herself it would go away.

What would Terri think of all of this? She had no idea. Terri had met Tom over Christmas break. They had gone out to dinner together.

"He's nice," Terri had commented after they got home.

"Oh, you think so. I mean, yes, he is."

"So, Mom, what's happening? Are you two serious?"

"Oh no, not at all. Not yet anyway. I don't know. But what about you? What about you and your boyfriend? What's happening with you?"

"Oh, not much to tell. In fact, we are more just friends than anything. I mean I like him and all, but . . ."

"But what?"

"I don't know, you know. He's nice but . . ."

"No sparks?" Inside Kate gave a sigh of relief.

"He has a girlfriend, Mom," Terri paused. "I miss home . . ."

"You can always come back," Kate assured her.

"What about, 'If you are going to do this I want you to give it a fair chance. Give it a year?'"

"Must have been out of my mind. You wouldn't hold a crazy woman to her word, would you?" Kate made a face to convince Terri both of her craziness then and her sanity now.

"No, you were right. This was something I had to do for myself. I need to see it through, or at least give it a fair chance."

"You can always change your mind. Woman's prerogative, remember."

"I know. I'm tired. Guess it's time for bed." Kate watched her walk up the stairs. How she missed her. How she still missed her. What would Terri say about Frank? She doesn't have to know everything. There are some things that are best that daughters don't know. Still she wished now that Terri had met him, or at least knew he existed. It would make him seem more real. Despite their time together he still seemed like a phantom from her past, not haunting her, but not letting her rest either.

X

It had been almost three months since that terrible night. She remembered it like it was yesterday. The memory played over and over in her head for weeks afterwards. The pain. The guilt. If only, she thought. If only they hadn't been out in the sun so much that day. If only he hadn't insisted on snorkeling. If only she had insisted he rest during the day. The doctors reassured her there had been nothing she could have done to prevent the stroke. If not that day, then the next. It had just been a matter of time. There was no way of knowing it would happen. He had appeared to be in good health, showed no signs of any problems at his last doctor's appointment. Sometimes these things just happen.

"If only I had insisted on a full physical before we left," Helen agonized to her daughters.

"Mom, stop it. You heard what the doctors said. There was no way of knowing."

"But I should have seen the warning signs."

"Stop it, Mom. Stop blaming yourself. That's the last thing Dad would want. Just be grateful he's alive." Allyson and Lindsey had repeated over and over and eventually she almost believed it.

There had been that terrible helicopter flight off the boat to the hospital. Fortunately they had been able to get him to a hospital in Florida. Then those anxious days when she didn't know whether he was going to make it and if he did make it the extent of the damage. He had had a stroke. That was all she knew. He was still alive, that she also knew, but would he make it? And if he made it, would he still be the man she had married? Would he remember her? Would he survive with his memory intact? She had known of stroke survivors who had a complete change of personality. Some for better, others for worse. Mild-mannered, easy-going men who had become grouchy, even violent. Grouchy, irritable men who had become easy-going. She didn't want any change. She just wanted him back.

It had been a relief when her daughters had finally made it to sit with her during those hours when he was in intensive care. They had stayed with her for those first few weeks, until he was well enough to be transferred to a rehabilitation facility closer to home. There he had spent three months, regaining much of what he had lost. There she had also spent three months of her life, driving back and forth every day.

The stroke had affected the right side of his body, left side of his brain. He had to slowly relearn how to walk, how to talk, how to feed himself, dress himself, clean himself. And she needed to learn how to help him with this, what she needed to do for him, what she needed to let him do. But he was still there, the man she remembered was still locked in a body that wouldn't allow him to communicate. She could see it in his eyes if not hear it in his voice.

"I don't want to lose you," she had whispered to him in the quiet of his room in intensive care, before her daughters had arrived. "Please don't leave me now that we've finally found each other again, after all these years. Please don't leave me now. We have a lot more life ahead of us. You are my future. I've been feeling lost all these years since the kids have left home. I've been feeling I had no future. That I had lost my future. I had nothing to live for, nothing to dream for. I wasn't about to be proclaimed the World's Greatest Teacher, wasn't to go much further there. I had thought maybe my future was in community service and politics, but that too was a dead end.

"But now I know, you are my future. You are my past, my present, my future. We were meant to grow old together. Please don't take my future away from me. Please don't leave me when we have so much to live for," she had told him in the quiet of the room, in the dark of the night, when no one was around. She had prayed and hoped someone was listening. She hoped and prayed Don would understand.

That had been almost three months ago. Slowly, day by day, she was starting to plan again, to dream of a future together.

"Don't live for me," Don had slowly written with his left hand one day.

"What?" she had said, struggling to read the scrawl.

He pointed at the words, unable to say them.

"I'm not living for you. You must live for me," she had told him, but she had known what he meant.

Other times he had written, "Go home," when he had seen how tired she was.

"I don't want to go home. I want to stay with you, make sure everything is okay."

"Go home," he had pointed at the paper and then wrote, "Okay." She had wanted to argue with him but even in his weakened state, he was still a force to be reckoned with.

"Don't make me future. Live life," he wrote another time.

"You heard me?!" she said. His eyes said, yes. "You heard me that day in ICU?" Again his eyes said yes as he squeezed her hand with his good hand. And she knew then, he would be okay, they would be okay.

"You are my future, my past, my present," she restated.

He pointed again at what he had written. She smiled and squeezed his hand gently. She knew what he meant. She knew she could start to make plans again.

He had made considerable progress over those three months. He would continue to need therapy but was strong enough to come home. She had arranged for a ramp so he could be brought inside in his wheelchair, but he had insisted on walking up the ramp using his walker. His right leg still dragged, but the hope was he'd be able to walk with a cane eventually. His speech was slow but understandable. He struggled to write with his right hand, however he had become quite good at using his left hand. His smile and sense of humor remained the same. With work, over time, the only remaining sign of his stroke would be the slight limp in his right leg. The prognosis was good for a full recovery.

With only a few months left in her sabbatical, Helen was making plans to return to teaching in the fall, but at a slower pace than she had in the past. The teacher who had filled in for her freshman Philosophy classes had been retained on the faculty. He would continue to teach freshman and sophomore classes, leaving her more time to teach upper level and graduate classes. She was looking forward to the change, looking forward to getting back to the classroom. There was still some interest on her part and the Republican Party's part in her running again, but that was for the future, not right now. A maybe, in a few years, not a yes.

For now her yes was to being home, watching her husband's progress. Her yes was to being alive, enjoying each day, each moment she had, storing up memories for the future.

Your old men shall dream dreams.
Joel 3:1

XI

He woke up to the sound of birds. Pre-dawn sunlight was just starting to creep over the horizon. He had no need for an alarm clock, no need to get up at a set time every day. He had long been retired. Still he woke up with the birds, if not before then, most days. Even those days he woke up at 2 a.m. and couldn't get back to sleep till four, he still woke up with the birds. Rarely did he sleep beyond 6 a.m., usually up by five and ready for a nap by 9 a.m. or earlier. Such was his life in retirement, in these "golden" years. Didn't feel too golden to him.

Arthritis made just getting out of bed an accomplishment. He forced himself to get up, get moving and keep moving lest he lose what strength and flexibility he still had. He walked a mile or two every day, more on days he didn't make it to the Y to swim. He guessed he was still in somewhat good shape. Cataracts made his vision cloudy, like opening his eyes underwater. His crystal-clear, twenty-twenty vision with which he had been such a crack shot during the war, a crack shot at hunting as well, was long gone. Those days were over, he thought, so leave the hunting to younger men with better vision. He had yet to give up fishing. So relaxing to go out in his son's boat or just sit along the shore, but not too long before stiffness started to set in. Still those days fishing were good days.

He still had good days, days when it didn't hurt so much to move; days with something to fill the time rather than keeping the TV on all day for company and listening to the depressing state of the world. No news was good news. All the news he heard was bad. Another war. More young men, and now young women, being sent to war, coming home maimed if not physically, then emotionally.

He certainly knew about that. Sixty years since his days in World War II, still just as fresh as yesterday. He had only been nineteen when he had enlisted for the war, he and his best buddy, Bob. They had hoped to be sent to the Pacific Theater. After Pearl Harbor they had been bent on getting some Japs. But instead they

110

had ended up in Europe, joining in the efforts to free France of German Rule. How long ago that had been and yet like yesterday.

So funny now to see France and Germany working together as part of the European Union. So funny that now we were allies not only with Germany, but Japan as well. So funny and strange. What short memories it seemed, or maybe it was just that we had to learn to live together or we would die together. We couldn't afford the luxury of nursing hatred, bitter blood feuds that extended for generations like the Hatfields and McCoys. The world had changed. This was to have been the war to end all wars, wasn't it, or had that been WWI? Couldn't remember. Next World War would certainly be the one to end all wars because the world wouldn't survive it. Not with nuclear weapons. He just prayed this mess in the Middle East wouldn't escalate any further. Yes, no news was good news. Sometimes better to turn it off.

He remembered so well being part of the invasion force in Normandy. He shot almost blindly it seemed, slowly advancing with Bob at his side. They had joked about celebrating in Paris, maybe finding some grateful French women, certainly drinking French wine.

His good eyes had served him well, kept him alive but not good enough. During the final advance, when they had the enemy on the run, he saw Bob was no longer with him.

"Bob," he had shouted and looked to either side, but he couldn't go back right then. He had had to keep moving forward, praying that Bob was moving forward as well. It was only after the shooting had ceased that he had been able to find him, but it had been too late. Too late to save him, too late to even say goodbye for Bob was already among the dead.

If only he had gone back the minute he had noticed Bob was gone. If only he had stayed closer to him, kept him within his range of vision, maybe he could have saved him, or maybe it would have been him hit rather than Bob. That would have been better.

But he was a soldier and not allowed to dwell on such thoughts, nor allowed to grieve. There was work yet to be done. When the work was done there would be time for such thoughts and to grieve.

He had marched into Paris amidst cheers and song. VE day! The wine was plentiful, as were the women, but Jim couldn't enjoy either. He had seen too much already in his young life. It had been only the thought of his fiancé, waiting for him, that got him through to the end. He lived to see her, to be with her once again and put thoughts of war behind him.

He had lived to see his beautiful Linda - que linda, how pretty. Her name meant "pretty" in Spanish and beautiful she had been with her auburn hair and brown eyes. She had been the most beautiful sight he had ever seen coming down that aisle in white, his beautiful bride. She had been a balm for his eyes, a sight to blot out visions of death, a cure for his heart, broken by the loss of his best buddy and other friends. But it hadn't been enough to blot out the memories or to heal the hurt. Six months out of the military he had been plagued by recurring nightmares. He would thrash about in the middle of the night.

He feared hurting his young wife and so would move to the couch where his nightmare would remain his own. She would come out and call his name, "Jim, what's wrong? Come back to bed." One time she reached over and touched him on the shoulder. He jumped and pulled his fist, prepared for a fight. Then he saw her face. He caught himself in time, that time. She never bothered him while he slept again.

He had had Post Traumatic Stress Syndrome before they had a name for it. All he could do was tough it out, work hard during the day, fall exhausted into bed and hope to sleep without dreams.

Still there had been good times. The nightmares lessened over time. Through it all his wife had stayed by his side. They had raised three children and had made a good life for themselves. He considered himself blessed. But then their youngest son had been killed in a tragic car accident as a teenager. He didn't know what was worse, his own grief or seeing how it had hurt his wife, tore her apart from the inside out. This time she was the one who couldn't sleep, roaming through the house at night, sitting in her son's old bedroom.

The nightmares reoccurred and he had had to be admitted into the VA hospital psych ward. It was there that his PTSD had been diagnosed and treatment begun. They put him on a medication to help him sleep through the night and sent him back home to his grieving Linda. Somehow they had managed to pull through this tragedy with their marriage still intact, but it had been hard. Then their daughter had died of cancer. Five years later his wife joined their daughter, also a cancer victim, although he believed she had died from a broken heart. There was only so much loss a heart could handle.

That had been five years ago. He didn't know why he was still around. He saw no reason for him remaining. Once again, someone he had loved had been taken from him, leaving him behind. He had been left behind during WWII, left behind when his son had died. He should have died, not Greg. And he had been left behind by his wife and daughter.

He didn't understand what God was keeping him around for. He had nothing to live for, no reason for being. His greatest reason for being, his wife, had been taken from him. Now he got up each day, walked his miles, swam his laps, but all for no reason. He longed to be with his wife again, with his son and daughter and buddy. Too many layers of grief piled on one after the other, a life time of grief. It was too much for anyone to bear. He wished God would take him home instead of leaving him here.

Still he had his oldest son and his wife, who had become like a daughter to him. He had his grandchildren. His son had two children, a son in college, daughter in high school. He and Eva had married later in life and postponed children. He had three strapping grandsons from his daughter, and his son-in-law who had remained close, like another son. It had been his son-in-law who had followed in his footsteps, taking over the construction business he had built up over the years when he had been ready to retire. He guessed he had these blessings for his older years, a reason to live, but it wasn't enough. How he missed his wife these past five years. She had died just short of their fiftieth wedding anniversary. Fifty years of his life with this one beautiful woman, still not enough.

"Grandpa, did you always want to work in construction?" he remembered his grandson asking him four months ago when he was home for Christmas.

"What do you mean by always? Always is a long time?" he had asked in reply.

"I mean, when you were my age, did you know what you wanted to do? Did you know when you were a teenager?"

"Hmm, let me think about that one, so long ago . . ." and yet he remembered those years better than he remembered what he had eaten for breakfast. "I guess I always knew I wanted to build things. I wanted to build something great, do something great, like build the Taj Mahal, or at least the Empire State building. I wanted to be an architect, not just any architect but a great one, another Frank Lloyd Wright."

"So what happened?"

"What happened? The war happened first, but actually that opened doors. I went off to war, then came home and went to college on the GI bill. Of course by then I was married to your grandmother, and then your uncle came along. I had the opportunity to work full time at the construction company I had worked at during summers in high school. It was good pay. The owner liked me, liked the fact I had some college education. I figured, why go to school to do something I was already doing, building? So I quit school, got an associate degree, but never became an architect, never designed any great monuments, but I built some pretty nice buildings right here in town where I can see them every day.

"Got to build that whole subdivision you live in. After the war all those soldiers came home, got married and along came the kids. They all needed homes to live in. I had a good opportunity to get in on the ground floor of the housing boom stemming from the baby boom. Eventually my boss made me partner and when he retired I bought him out. I didn't build anything great, but I did build a good business that provided a needed service to the community and provided for a good life for my family. Maybe I didn't build the Sears Tower or anything like it, but I built a good life for myself and my family and my grandkids. Why do you ask?"

"I just wanted to know. You know, all through high school they keep asking you – what do you want to do with your life? It's like it's the only conversation starter anyone knows. And so I've had to come up with something. And before I knew it, I kind of believed the story I was telling everyone. But now I'm in college and I don't know what I want to do. I guess I'd like to do something, something, if not great, at least special. I just don't know what."

"So going into the family business doesn't appeal to you?"

114

"Not that much, I guess. Not that it's not good work or a good way to make a living. It's just not for me. I want to do more than that. I want to do more than just make a living, do you understand?"

Sure he understood. Was it actually seventy years since he had been a teenager too, full of life and ambition? Where had it gone? Had he achieved any of the grand accomplishments, grand adventures he had hoped for and dreamed of? Had he traveled to all of the countries he had wanted to explore when young? No, he had traveled during the war and that had been enough. Nothing like traveling during war time, seeing buildings and people blown away, to make you appreciate home. He wondered, had that been when his dreams had been destroyed, buried somewhere in northern France? Or had it been a slow death over the years?

One by one they had gone, dropped out of his radar, perhaps with the birth of each child. But he hadn't lost all of his dreams. They had just been altered. He had dreamed of building and that he had done. Hardly an office building in the area that his company hadn't worked on at one time or another, even if they had not build it from the ground up. And all of the homes he had built.

He could have gone on to be an architect back in his fifties when the business was going strong and his son-in-law had come on board and taken over some of his responsibilities. He could have gone back to school then, but by then he no longer felt the desire to design buildings. He had been content with what he had built, content with his life, and had wanted to just ride out the remainder of his years, take it easier, be able to take a trip now and then with Linda. He had looked forward to retirement and spending winters in Florida. Going back to school had just not interested him then.

He had new dreams then, dreams of a peaceful retirement. And he had realized those dreams as well. While he hadn't retired completely until he was sixty-two, he had cut back significantly before then, joining the ranks of the snow birds who flew south every winter by the time he hit sixty. They had been good years for him and his wife. Enjoying the fruits of their labor, enjoying their grandchildren, enjoying more time with friends, going on cruises in the Caribbean, a cruise to Alaska, flying to Hawaii for the honeymoon they had never had.

But then the unthinkable had happened: Their daughter became ill. They came back from Florida to help in any way they could, curtailed their travel plans in order to be available to help. Jim went back to work part-time so his son-in-law could go to doctor appointments with his wife. Linda had stepped in to help with their kids. It had been a five-year, roller coaster ride, with times of remission when they had thought it was beat, but just as they returned to some semblance of normalcy, some resemblance of their former life, there had been a recurrence. His wife along with other family members had provided around-the-clock nursing care for the last few months of her life.

It had seemed like they were barely back to normal, barely functioning again, had hardly adjusted to Laura being gone, when his wife had found a lump in her breast. It all began again. Another five years of chemo, radiation, remission and recurrence. Another roller coaster ride, only this time, at the end, he was all alone, without his wife who had spent more years with him than he had spent without her. How could he go on without her? This couldn't be happening. So much for the golden years. How could the years be golden without her by his side to share them?

He had never imagined that this would happen. Had always assumed he would be the first to go. Didn't women normally live longer than men? This went against the statistics. He didn't fit the statistics, nor did he fit anywhere any more. He didn't feel like he belonged, not here in this house where they had raised their family, not in this town where he had grown up, not in this world. He didn't belong anywhere without her. He had prayed that God would take him. If he was a merciful God, certainly he would take him, put him out of his misery, but God wasn't merciful and so he remained, and so had passed another five years of not living.

His kids had tried to talk him into moving out of this big house and moving in with them, or if not that, then into one of the retirement communities newly populating the area.

"Come on, Dad, you built them, you might as well enjoy them. We worry about you alone in that big house."

Let someone else enjoy those buildings. He was going to stay put. How could he move? How could he sort through a lifetime of "stuff" and decide what to leave behind and what to take? How could he leave the memories? At first they had haunted him at

116

every turn, but now they were a comfort to him. How could he leave the rose bushes she had tended for so many years? He had taken over their care during the last months of her life, bringing fresh cut flowers in to her room each morning. How could he leave those behind? And yet finally he had agreed to move. Their two-story, four-bedroom house was more than he could handle. He had basically only been living in a few rooms on the first floor, leaving the upstairs to the cobwebs.

So he downgraded to a two-bedroom ranch, all on one floor. He carefully chose what to bring with him, the dining room table and chairs, sofa and his recliner, her rocker. Everything else was given away. He had managed to transplant one of her rose bushes and start a small garden, tomatoes, green peppers, corn, just enough to keep him busy and outside in the fresh air.

In some ways it had been a relief to move. Much less painful to feel he didn't belong here than to remain in the house that had once been home but that was no longer home. It had been a good life, his life with her. Would he ever feel at home again without her, even after five years?

God hadn't been merciful. God hadn't put him out of his misery. God had left him to live, once again. He didn't know why. He didn't know why he was still alive when so many others had died. He didn't know why he didn't put an end to his life himself; do what God wouldn't do for him. But he didn't. Somehow he couldn't bring himself to do it. Maybe it was because he was just a coward. Whatever the reason, God wouldn't put him out of his misery, and he couldn't do it either, and so he lived. Slowly days went by. A new sense of normalcy developed, whatever that meant. He lived one day at a time and slowly, he started to live again.

He met old friends over breakfast every Thursday. Over the years members had come and gone, till now there were only four regulars, friends he had known most of his life, business associates and now friends. They met, talked about inconsequential things, other friends, hunting and fishing, local politics, local gossip. It was all good.

Other mornings he would dig in his garden, weed around his tomato plants, tend to Linda's rose bushes. This too was good. It was good to have his hands in the dirt, feel connected to earth. It was good to be outside, good to watch new life take shape day by day in front of his eyes. Good to see blossoms bloom and turn into food for his table. Good to be part of all of this.

Memories of childhood came back to his mind as he dug in the dirt: memories of his mother and grandmother. How his mother had tended to their garden. Hours he had spent weeding the family garden as a child.

"Jimmy, come over here," his mother called, wiping sweat from her forehead. "Let me show you how it's done." He squatted next to her, smelling sweat and earth. "See, these small shoots right here?"

"This?" he reached out and touched the green.

"Yes, that's the carrot, everything else is weed. You have to pick the weeds and leave the carrot. Do you think you can do it?"

He nodded his head. He felt important, being trusted with a job.

"Okay, you work on the carrots while I weed around the potatoes." It had seemed like fun for about ten minutes.

"What's the matter?" his mother asked.

"I don't want to pick weeds anymore. I'm hot," his six-year-old self whined.

His dad, coming out of the barn on his way to the house for a cool drink, overheard him. "What's this about being too hot? I'm not raising any babies. If your mother can work in the hot sun, then so can you. You get back to work."

"It's all right, James. He's just a child. He'll work now, won't you, Jimmy?"

"You think this is hard, you come out to the barn. I'll show you what hard work is."

"You go on, get yourself something to drink and leave the garden to Jimmy and me, right Jimmy?" Jimmy shook his head yes. He knew he had it better with his mother than working with his brothers and dad. Still he would see other kids from school playing and envy them their freedom. Sometimes his mother would say, "Finish that row and then you can go play." Then Jim would fly through the row in order to join his friends. Other times there was no let up. What Jim hadn't known at the time was that his friends often went to bed hungry. They envied him and his garden and the milk in abundance they always had from the cows.

118

Sometimes his mother would slip them some of their vegetables. A carrot could be a wonderful treat to someone who is hungry.

Then it had seemed pure torture, stuck doing this chore while his friends were riding bikes, getting into trouble. But that garden had been all that had kept food on their table during the depression years. He guessed he should have been grateful for the blessing of food when so many had so little. Food always appeared on the table, thanks to his mother's garden and his father's hard work caring for the dairy.

How he had wanted to be away from all of this. The last thing he had wanted was to follow in his father's footsteps, be a dairy farmer, milking cows, pasteurizing milk. He had longed to move far away, see sights he had never seen, maybe fly in an airplane like Lucky Lindy – anything to escape the dirt and smells of the farm.

Now here he was, his hands deep in dirt, enjoying the memories it brought. Funny how different the world looks now, how detested chores of childhood are comforts in old age. How it had taken him a life-time to come full circle and finally know the blessings that were his. That garden and those cows had provided a better life for him and his brothers. His brothers were gone. They had been the ones to take on the family dairy until they had been bought out by a much larger operation. Being the youngest son, he had been relegated to work in the garden with his mother and grandmother, women's work he had disdainfully thought back then. Still better than the smelly barn and milking cows.

And he remembered. Funny what he remembered. Funny how his mind jumped around from one memory to the next, seemingly unconnected. His once-disciplined mind was every bit as undisciplined as his body had become. He could no longer trust it to remember with accuracy dates and names, appointments. He wrote everything in his calendar to assist him. Linda used to be his calendar, his own personal secretary, she used to say.

"Jim, you'd forget your head if it wasn't attached to your neck, if you didn't have me around. What would you do without me?"

"I hope I never have to find out," he had said. So now he had found out. He had to work to keep his head on straight, but slowly it was coming. Slowly he was learning. "I guess I'd have to hire a real secretary," he had said.

"Who would put up with you!" she had retorted with a smile. "You are my full-time job."

How his thoughts slipped around in his mind, first here, then there, jumping from one decade to the next with no rhyme or reason. Was his brain trying to figure something out? If so, he didn't know what. Maybe he was trying to make some sense of his life.

It had been a good life. Could have been better, could have been worse, over all it was his, his life. He had lived it the best he could. There were some dreams left unfulfilled, but nothing important. Nothing he hadn't been willing to leave behind him. If there was something left undone, he didn't know what it was. Which was all the more reason to wonder why God kept him around. He didn't know of any unfinished business keeping him here. And so he lived from day to day.

Funny how he had outlived so many of his friends, outlived all of his family of his generation, except for his one sister-in-law. She was in a nursing home in Florida, her mind far away, long gone thanks to dementia. He and Linda had used to visit her each winter while staying in Florida, but then she had moved into the nursing home and their stays in Florida grew fewer and far between. Now the most contact he had from her was a card at Christmas and a phone call update from his niece who lived in Florida, close to her mother.

He had more friends in the next life than he had in this life. It hadn't been a bad life. It felt . . . complete. There was only one thing left and that was death.

"I'm ready any time you are," he said, but when God didn't answer he got up, made his bed and put on the coffee.

He didn't know why God didn't take him home. "I guess I'm just too ornery," he thought.

Then he heard a knock on the door. Slowly he made his way to the door, opened it and was surprised by a woman carrying a pie.

"Welcome, neighbor. I live across the street. I brought you a house-warming gift." She stood on his porch, holding the pie in front of her, waiting for Jim to respond. "Can I come in?" she

120

finally asked as Jim stood mute, unsure what to say. She moved past him to the kitchen.

"Here," she said, placing the pie on the table. "It's still warm. Care for a piece?" she asked as she looked in the cupboards for a plate.

"What are you doing?" Jim asked.

"Looking for plates. You can't eat pie with your fingers."

"Here," he said as he pushed past her to the cupboard and handed her a plate.

"Now where do you keep your silverware?" she asked, pulling out drawers. "I need a knife to cut the pie and a fork."

Jim handed her a knife and pulled out a fork for himself.

She cut him a piece, set it down in front of him, pointing to him to sit down, then sat down herself.

"By the way, my name is Bess."

We live as we dream - alone.
Joseph Conrad, Heart of Darkness

XII

The smell of death hung heavy about her. No one else noticed, but she did. She could feel death in the air though thousands of miles away. It was as real as the crow sitting on the wire outside of her window. The smell perched on her shoulder and followed her around wherever she went, at work, at play, while she ate, while she slept. The world had been tense, too, during these first days of fighting. We knew it was coming, knew it would be soon, and then the day arrived. The TV showed air attacks at night as the world watched. Kate had watched as well, knowing that somewhere behind all that aircraft maneuvering was her Frank, her beloved. Death seemed so real, filling her dreams, waking her at night in a sweat.

The days went on. There were casualties, but not too many. Still her fears were unabated. Any doubt in her mind about her future, their future, dissolved in her worry. "Dear God, just bring him home safe. That's all I want," she prayed each day. "I'll do whatever you want. I'm ready to give up everything, move to D.C., if that's what you want, if only to be with him." Thoughts of Tom faded out of her mind. She was prepared to make a new start, somewhere else, with a new love, if only God would spare his life.

What did she have to hold her there? She had a house, nothing more, no-one to share it with. She had a job and friends, but she could get a new job and make new friends. She was still young enough for that. She pushed back the clouds of worry and focused on her work to get her through each day, till that fateful call in the beginning of May, confirmed by accounts in the news. The war was over, so soon, what a relief.

"When will you be coming home?" Kate asked between tears.

"We've got some mopping up to do yet. That could take some time. Still, I might be able to get back to the USA as early as June."

"That would be wonderful. I miss you."

"Miss you, too, babe. I've got to go. The line is dying." She heard him say over the static. Maybe June, maybe June, she thought. He's safe. He'll be home soon. What a relief. Kate began to make plans in her head for her future, their future.

Frank hung up the phone and decided to get out of the command center. Too much time spent behind a desk, he thought to himself. Too easy to send others off on combat missions while he sat in relative comfort and security, the thought weighed on him. Frank didn't like it. He was glad it would soon be over. This time when he left he wouldn't be returning. This time he would retire for good and build a new life for himself far from the roar of combat. Let others order young men and women into war to die. He had had enough of it, had done his duty and was ready to enjoy a new life with Kate.

So far all had gone relatively well, but even with that, there were casualties. Captain Chris Seifert and Major Gregory Stone had been among the early losses, killed by a hand grenade attack in Kuwait on March 22, only two days into fighting. There were more, so many more casualties, some dead, others maimed for life. You aim for as few casualties as possible, pray for the best, but he'd yet to see a mission without losses.

"I'm getting too old for this," he mumbled to no-one in particular as he picked himself up from his chair. He sealed the letter he had just written and placed it in the outgoing mail.

"What's all the noise?" he asked the sergeant who had just returned.

"Didn't you know? President Bush is flying in to announce the end of the war. Aren't you going on deck?"

"Oh, that explains it. Sure, I'll be out in a few minutes." The sergeant hurried back. Frank proceeded to the flight deck, skirting the crowds gathered. He didn't feel like celebrating, didn't think he deserved any share in the recognition. After all, he had not been putting his life on the line flying over enemy territory. Let the real heroes get the recognition they deserve, he thought.

He walked over to where a helicopter was being loaded.

"What are you doing?" he asked the pilot. "How come you aren't taking part in the festivities?"

"Can't. I have to air lift these medical supplies," he explained while examining his check list.

"How many missions have you flown since deployment?"

"Oh, I don't know. I stopped counting after twenty," he said as he checked to make sure the supplies were secure.

"Look, why don't you let me take this run. Would do me good to get off this ship for a while. You go and enjoy yourself."

"I can't do that general."

"Sure you can, tell them it was an order. The lieutenant and I can handle this," he said pointing to the officer waiting in the helicopter.

"Go ahead, John, you deserve a break," he shouted in affirmation.

John paused before agreeing. "All right, who am I to disobey orders. It would be nice to have a break," he said while Frank climbed into the cockpit in his place. Frank smiled and saluted as the helicopter took off.

"Any word from Frank?" a familiar deep voice interrupted her thought as she walked through the grocery store.

"Hi, Tom. Yes, in fact he's safe and hopes to be back soon."

"That's great news," Tom said sincerely.

"It is," Kate agreed. "It was kind of you to ask." An awkward silence ensued. "It's great to see you. You're looking good."

"You look good too," Tom said. "Guess I better be going. It was good to see you," he said as he turned to leave.

"Good to see you, too," Kate repeated quietly to herself. It was good. It's always good to see friends. Kate reminded herself of that. That's all it was, nothing more. Still she felt a certain sadness inside. Choices can be so hard sometimes. But the thought of Frank alive chased away her sadness.

The message light on her answering machine was blinking when she got home.

"Mrs. Connors? This is Lieutenant Chad Shaughnessy, Frank Shaughnessy's son. We met in D.C. . . . . I'll call you later."

What was that about, Kate wondered? Was something wrong? Was Frank hurt? Why didn't he call himself? A deep pain seared across her chest and into the pit of her stomach. If only he had left a number for her to call. She'd call him back right away and end this unknowing. Maybe he was hurt. That's it. He's hurt but he'll be okay. He'll be coming home soon. That has to be the reason for the call. But then, why didn't Frank call himself? Because he's too hurt to call, that's why.

Kate had no idea how long it took until the phone finally rang. Only it wasn't Chad. It was Terri.

"Hi Mom, you got a minute?"

"I guess. I'm expecting a call. What's up?" Kate was too distraught to catch the anxiety in Terri's voice.

"Mom, you know, if it's okay with you, I think I'd like to move back home with you."

"Of course it's all right. Any time. You know this is still your home. Are you okay?"

"I'm okay. It's just, oh, everything, I guess. I just want to come home."

"That's nice, dear. I'll have to call you later. I've got another call coming in," Kate cut Terri off in order to take the call. Terri stared in amazement at her phone. What was that all about? She expected her mom to want to talk over everything, and over and over and over.

"Mrs. Connors?"

"Yes, this is Kate," Kate's stomach jumped at the familiar voice, so like Frank's.

"Kate, this is Chad Shaughnessy."

"I could tell. You sound so much like your dad. How is he?"

"That's why I'm calling. He told me if anything happened to him to call you. You were important to him."

"Is he all right? Is he hurt? I just spoke to him a day ago. What happened?"

"I'm sorry. I'm afraid he . . . he's dead. It was a surprise thing. No one thought there was any real danger. He was helping to airlift some medical supplies to a hospital. Not really something he was required to do, but something he wanted to do. He wanted to give the helicopter pilot a break. It was shot down and my dad with it."

Kate didn't know what to say. "He's dead? He can't be. He told me he would be home soon. This can't be real."

"I wish it wasn't. I wish to God it wasn't real. It's all a nightmare," Chad's voice broke into tears.

"I'm sorry. This must be terrible for you too. I just can't believe it right now. What about the funeral?"

"It'll be a week or so before we can get the body back stateside. He'll be buried in Arlington cemetery next to my grandfather. I'm sorry for your loss."

"For all of us. It's your loss as well."

"I'll let you know when the funeral will be as soon as I know. I got to go now. I'm sorry."

Kate slowly returned the receiver to the phone. It wasn't possible. She jumped when the phone rang again. It wasn't true, she told herself. It was just a crazy prank, a cruel joke. This next call would be Frank. It had to be Frank, but it was Terri.

"Mom, did you hear what I said? I want to move back home."

"I did Terri. Of course I did."

"Don't you want to talk about it?"

"Now's not a good time. I'll call you later," Kate said and hung up the phone. She sat down in a state of shock, staring at the phone. She didn't feel anything. It was all too unreal. It couldn't be true, couldn't have happened.

She turned on the TV only to see the news. More reports about the war, the end of the war, pillaging in the cities and villages, looting. Two helicopters on humanitarian missions to bring much needed medical supplies to a hospital had been shot down. No names were being released pending notification of their families. No—this just in, one of the pilots was General Frank Shaughnessy. Not the usual place for a general to be.

They showed someone who knew Frank saying how this was just the kind of leader he always was. He never asked anything of those under his command that he wasn't willing to do himself. He had told the pilot to take a break, that he would fly the mission for him. Then in front of her eyes, for all the world to see, was his picture, Frank Shaughnessy Jr. Her Frank. She still couldn't believe it. She ignored the phone the next time it rang. Let her answering machine pick it up, she thought.

"Kate, it's me, Tom. I just saw the news. Kate, are you all right? Call me." But Kate didn't call. She continued to sit and stare at the TV without really seeing anything as it grew dark outside all around her.

"Kate, if you're there, pick up. Are you okay?" Tom called back but Kate still didn't respond. She didn't answer when she heard the doorbell. She just continued to sit. She didn't get up when she heard the door open. She didn't move as Tom moved slowly next to her.

"Kate, I had to come see if you were okay. Are you okay?" he asked tentatively.

"No, I'm not okay. Nothing will ever be okay anymore. I don't know what to say. What do I do now? It hurts too much to cry. If I cry then it will be real. It's not real. It's all a cruel hoax."

"Can I fix you something to eat? Get you something to drink? Is there anything I can do?"

"Just hold me, please, hold me. Don't leave me, not right now." Tom sat down next to her and held her.

"I won't leave you. I'm here for you," he stated quietly.

The next week was a blur. Tom accompanied her to Washington for the funeral. What made it all the harder was that hardly anyone had known about her relationship with Frank. She was there but it felt like she didn't belong. There was his former wife, his son, his sister and her family, his mother. The only one who even had known she had existed was his son. He came over and thanked her for coming. She was so grateful for Tom's support. It had been awkward asking for the time off from work. She had to tell her boss and co-workers but no one else in town knew about her loss. Her parents didn't even know. Terri had figured it out after seeing the news, but didn't know the whole story.

"Mom, was that the guy you had been dating while I was gone?"

"Yes, it was."

"Are you all right? Do you want me to come out there?"

"I'm okay. You finish out your school year. I'll be okay." What could Terri do or say at a time like this. Not much, she was afraid. She just had to get through it. She was grateful for Tom's quiet presence. He seemed to know quiet was what she needed more than anything. Not a lot of idle talk. He waited till she was ready to talk.

"You ready?" he had asked as she had said her final goodbye at the graveside. They had come back after everyone had left.

"As ready as I'll ever be, I guess," Kate said as she allowed him to lead her back to the car.

"Wait," she said and turned around, "Can I just have a couple minutes more, alone?"

"Sure, I'll wait in the car."

Kate walked back to the grave. "I guess this is goodbye. I can't lose you again, Frank. I lost you once, two times is just more than any woman can bear. I know, you'll always be with me in spirit, but spirit can't hold me at night or wipe away my tears or laugh at my jokes. I want a real life, flesh and blood love in my life, not a ghost, not a memory, not just a dream. Sometimes it seems like a dream. Just one of many dreams that didn't quite happen.

"I suppose thirty years from now I'll still remember you. I won't forget any more than I forgot that summer we had, but it will all be in the past, a lifetime ago. I just have to get through it. And I can love again, can't I? You would want that. I've got to let you go, and you've got to let me go. I want to be free to love again, to dream again even if those dreams are for naught, even if they all evaporate into the mist or end up buried in the cold hard ground of a cemetery like our dreams of a future were. I have to dream again. Help me be free to dream again."

She bent down to touch his gravestone then stood up, finally ready to leave.

"Guess I won't be moving to D.C. after all," Kate commented after driving for miles in silence.

"You weren't really serious about moving, were you?" Tom questioned.

"I don't know. Seemed like a good idea at the time."

"What does D.C. have that we don't?" Tom teased, hoping to lighten her mood.

"A chance for a future, a change. Something new and different. A new beginning," Kate said with her voice cracking and tears rising to the surface once again. Was she ever going to stop crying, she wondered?

"Did you know Terri's moving back home?" she changed the subject, still fighting tears.

"No, that's great news, isn't it?"

"Yes, it is," Kate said as tears began to flow again. She reached for the box of tissues on the back car seat. "It really is."

"You don't sound too happy."

"No, I am. I'm crazy. I really am happy. I don't know why I'm crying. When I first heard about Frank I couldn't cry at all. Now I can't stop. It really is great about Terri. I'll be happy to have her home."

"It's okay," Tom said, reaching across the driver seat to take her hand. "If you need to cry, it's okay, go ahead. I've got plenty of tissues."

"Thanks," Kate laughed slightly even while still sniffing back tears.

"Does Terri know about Frank?"

"Just a little. She knows I've been dating someone besides you."

"Is that why she's coming home?"

"No, she had decided this before she had heard the news. I guess she's just ready. She learned whatever it was she needed to learn and is ready to come home." Kate leaned her head back on the car seat, closing her eyes.

"We don't have to talk if you don't want to. We can ride in silence," Tom added as he squeezed her hand.

A man's reach must exceed his grasp, or what's a heaven for?
Robert Browning

XIII

True to her word, Terri came to the prom stag, her date being her camera. She had been asked by Sheri's brother who was home from college but Terri had felt it would have been a pity date and turned him down.

"Come on, Terri, Bryan's a good guy. You don't want to go to the prom alone," Sheri had insisted.

"What do you mean alone? I have my faithful companion, my Nikon. Someone has to chronicle the great event for all of you. After all . . ."

". . . It's not really my prom. I know, I know. You keep saying that. Suit yourself."

Terri walked out onto the deck in her prom dress, her camera swung around her neck. While others were going out to fancy restaurants for pre-prom dinners, she had decided to stay home. She didn't want to tag along with Sheri and her date. Instead she had called her mom to let her know her decision about the summer. Her mom had sounded kind of strange, like something was wrong, but she wouldn't say what.

Her dad joined her on the deck, watching the sun go down in the west and a few stars appearing in the east.

"Been a rough few weeks, hasn't it?"

"I guess so. Not really that bad, could have been worse."

"You going to leave?" He looked up at the stars.

"Do you want me to?" Terri also avoided looking at him, gazing off into the universe.

"No, of course not. You can stay as long as you want. What did your mom say?"

"She said it was up to me."

"Hard, isn't it, having to make all these decisions." This time he turned to face her.

"Yeah, I guess. It would have been easier if she had just told me to come home."

"But not better. I know she misses you. Must have been hard for her to let you come in the first place." When Terri didn't look at him he went back to star gazing.

"Yeah," Terri stared silently at the sky. "So Dad, how did all this happen?"

"All what?"

"All this, this house, this corporate lawyer bit. How did it happen? Weren't you going to change the world when you were younger?" This time it was Terri who turned to look at him, tossing back her long locks.

"Are you saying I'm a sell-out?" Dick smiled at her.

"No, yes, maybe. I just want to know what happened."

"Corporate lawyers can't change the world?" he teased.

"You know what I mean."

Dick paused before continuing, enjoying the cool breeze from the early evening air and listening to the fading sound of grasshoppers chirping in the dark. "I guess I don't really know how it happened, it just did, gradually, over time. First it was just the necessity of having a stable job to provide a decent living for my baby girl."

"Don't try to put this on me."

"I'm not. I'm not really sure what happened. I guess I just got tired of driving cars that kept breaking down, defending criminals who just kept coming back, revolving doors. Felt kind of futile. You know, not everybody who is poor and accused of a crime is innocent. Who says you have to be poor to change the world? I make a lot of money now, but I also give a lot of money away. I like to think, in my own way, I'm still making a difference." He turned and faced her, "you can make a difference, too. You're bright and full of ideas and enthusiasm. What do you want to do? What are your dreams?"

"I don't know. People keep asking me that, like I should know by now what I'm going to do with my life. I'm only sixteen. How can I know what I want to do with my life? I just want to live it."

"They're just trying to be polite, show some interest in you. What else do you say to a teenager to get a conversation going?"

"Anything but that." Terri turned away from him and back to the view. "Sometimes I think it would be great to travel the world taking pictures, maybe for National Geographic, or maybe join the

Peace Corps, build schools in countries without them. Or maybe study cultures like Margaret Mead."

"You can do any of these. The sky's the limit. Don't be afraid to reach for the stars."

"And if I fall."

"You pick yourself up and start again, just like you've done all this year. And remember, I'll be right there, cheering for you, me and all my corporate money. What better way to use that filthy lucre than helping my baby achieve her dreams? Remember how Gandhi said it cost his friends a lot of money to keep him in poverty."

Terri laughed.

"Sometimes life has a way of making choices for us, or at least altering our plans. Maybe that's what happened to me. I didn't necessarily lose my dreams; they were just altered through the process of living. Now I have different dreams."

"Like what?"

"Like seeing my baby girl graduate and go on to college and change the world."

"Yeah, like that's going to happen."

"You'd be surprised what can happen in a lifetime. Good things, always good things just waiting to happen, sometimes when you expect them the least. And when it doesn't work out how you expected, learn from them, make something good come out of it." He paused before continuing. "You know, I'm sorry about the move. Didn't mean to take you so far away from your home, your mother. It was just such a good deal, such a great opportunity. I just couldn't turn it down."

"That's all right, Dad. I mean, I was angry at first, but I love California. I'm glad I had the opportunity to live here. I just miss Mom and my friends and my dog. I want to go home. Maybe I'm not cut out to be a world traveler."

"What do you mean? Living in California is a whole different world from Ohio, and you made it for the whole year. Almost like studying abroad."

"And now it's time to go home."

"If you say so. I think you have a prom to go to first," he reminded her.

She drove herself to the prom. She was grateful for that. At least she didn't have to be dropped off by her dad. After an hour of taking shots of the Prom King and Prom Queen and all the happy couples, Terri was ready to call it a night. Perhaps she had been too hasty in turning down Sheri's brother, she thought to herself. Perhaps she had been too picky.

"Care for a dance?" She felt a light touch on her shoulder and turned around to face Josh.

"What about your date?"

"She went to the ladies room. Besides she won't mind. She knows we're friends."

"Yeah, friends. Sure, why not." Her camera banged against her chest. "Just a minute. Let me find a place for Nikki here." She found a spot on a table to set her camera, facing away from them. "He's very jealous. Best he not see us dancing."

Josh laughed as he escorted her out to the dance floor. "Having a good time? Wait, don't tell me."

"That obvious?"

"If it's any consolation, this hasn't exactly been the highlight of my school year." Terri looked up at him.

"Caroline and I are breaking up. We are both going to different schools next year and Caroline's got an internship in Washington for the summer that her mom, the senator, arranged for her so she won't be around all summer. Just seemed to make sense to break up now. We'll still go out till she leaves, or maybe not."

"I'm sorry to hear that."

"Really?"

"No, but it seemed the right thing to say."

"So what about you? Are you working at the country club this summer or going home?"

"Don't know. Don't really have any reason to stay."

"Maybe I could give you one."

Terri laughed and smiled back at him, "Maybe, but then I'm going back to my old high school and you're going off to college."

"We could still have the summer."

"Does that mean we might be more than friends?"

"Maybe."

"I'll think about it," Terri said as the dance ended.

XIV

"Grandpa," he heard the voice of Joy, his only granddaughter. "You're going to the parade, aren't you?"

"I don't know. Maybe not this year." He hadn't given it much thought. Was it actually Memorial Day again? How quickly one year faded into another.

"Yes, you are going. It wouldn't be the same without you. I'll be over to pick you up in twenty minutes."

"I can't possibly be ready in twenty minutes."

"That's all right. I'll help you," she had insisted.

How could he go to the Memorial Day Parade? All those years he never missed a parade, not even when his son had been born. He had gone from the hospital, too excited to rest, put on his uniform and marched, all the while his face gleaming because . . . he had a son! He was a father! Back then he had been accompanied by many other soldiers but over the years their number had dwindled.

Even as he got older and it became harder, even after the death of their youngest son when he had wanted to sit that one out, Linda had laid out his uniform for him. She had needed some sense of normalcy, he guessed and so he had gone along with it. She had had the suit let out by a tailor as he had gained his middle-aged spread and helped him with the buttons when his arthritis made it difficult.

Since her death he had to do this himself. He had decided to continue the ritual because it had lent some sense of normalcy to his upturned life. He had done it for her, in memory of her. When everything else had been taken away from him, at least this had remained. But this year he had thought it was time to quit. No reason to go. No one to walk with. There were so few of his generation left and those who were left couldn't walk that far. His grandchildren were no longer young enough to come and cheer him on, giving him a reason to walk. But apparently at least one grandchild would be there watching.

He reluctantly got his uniform out of the closet. It wasn't possible he could still wear it after all those years. It was threadbare in parts, held together by Linda's sewing. How he missed her. Certainly no one would know it if he missed this year's parade. How he wished he could back out of it. He slowly pulled on the pants and then the jacket. There was no way he would be able to button it by himself. That was why he avoided button-down shirts but opted for pullover shirts and sweaters, although he struggled with them as well.

"Grandpa, you ready?" he heard Joy let herself into the kitchen.

He walked out, his shirt open, sleeves un-cuffed.

"No, I can't fasten these guldarn buttons," he grumbled.

"Here, let me do it." She deftly buttoned his shirt and cuffed his sleeves. So much like her grandmother, he thought with a tear.

"You all right, Grandpa?" Joy asked.

"I'm fine. It's just you look so much like your grandmother when she was young. She was so beautiful." He paused, reached for his hat and added, "Guess we better be going."

"You look so handsome, Grandpa. I'm surprised some widow hasn't grabbed you up," she teased. He shook his head gruffly and headed out the door.

He still couldn't believe he was doing this. He was only doing it for his granddaughter. Only she could get him out into the hot sun. He refused to ride in the car they had for the World War II veterans.

"As long as I'm able to walk, I'll walk," he had insisted. "This is nothing. I walk several miles every day."

The parade was short, ran only halfway down Main Street to the cemetery and the War Memorial. There they listened to speeches praising veterans for their service to their country. Jim remembered Bob. Every year he added his own quiet prayer of remembrance to the multitude of words. Did anybody else remember Bob after all these years? Would anyone remember him sixty years from now when he was pushing up daisies? He doubted it. He'd long since be buried in some cemetery somewhere by then, long gone and forgotten.

It saddened him to see more generations of veterans, Korean War, Vietnam War, Gulf War and now the Iraq war. Would it ever end? Would we continue to send off future generations to fight future wars?

There was another group amidst the veterans, the Boy Scouts and Girl Scouts, DAR, high school band and drum and bugle corps. "Veterans for Peace," the sign said. Their number was small but noticeable. Some in the parade had taken offense at their presence and jeered at them. The soldiers did not respond in kind but quietly stood their ground until others had intervened, shushing the noisemakers and reminding them that these, too, had served their country and deserved to have their voice heard. Isn't that one of the freedoms they had fought to preserve?

It was a motley group, some in uniform, others in their civvies, some sporting T-shirts that read, "Another Veteran for Peace," or multi-colored peace signs. Some were hippie throwbacks from the Vietnam War era, others from the Gulf war. He found himself drawn to the group.

"So which war did you fight in?" one of the members asked him.

"World War II, the big one."

"Hey, thanks for doing that," he responded.

"Thank you, too. What war did you fight in?"

"Desert Storm, Gulf war, but you, you fought in the last war that had a good reason for us being in it."

Jim wasn't sure what to say to that. It was true. Hindsight was always better than foresight. Hitler truly had to be stopped and Japan had attacked us. Certainly generals and politicians always came up with good sounding reasons for being involved in wars but despite the noble words they might come up with such as keeping the world safe for democracy, fighting the red terror, more often than not it was about profit, greed and the lust for power. Not like the "big" war.

"So what does your group do?" Jim asked.

"We are just trying to let people know you can still be patriotic, still be a good American, serve your country and yet be against this war. That's all. We are not that organized. Having been through war ourselves, seen the horror of it, we just don't want to see any more men and women going through what we went through, especially not for this war."

"Don't you think it's too soon to say this war is wrong? After all, we did what President Bush had said we would. We got in there, moved fast and now just a few months later we have victory. Wouldn't you call it a success?"

"Would you? It's not over yet, not till all our troops come home."

"I guess I don't know yet. Time will tell."

"Unfortunately we may have lost many, many lives by then," he said as he prepared to leave. "It's been nice talking to you. If you ever care to join us, you are always welcome." He shook Jim's hand and handed him a flyer about their meetings.

"Hey, Dad," Tom affectionately called to his father-in-law. "You look great. It's always good to see you in your uniform." Tom was sincere in his comments. He'd been coming to the Memorial Day parade for years, since his marriage to Laura. It was a family tradition, going back to before she had been born when her dad had gone to the parade and watched his dad. She had been going since she was a baby in a stroller. In joining her family, he had accepted this tradition as well. Each year he and Laura had come for the parade, bringing their sons along.

He had skipped that first Memorial Day after Laura's death, but had been coaxed back into attending by his sons who had continued to enjoy the tradition. He had considered skipping this year, especially since Kate didn't want to attend. Tom's youngest son was home from college for the summer, but he was much more interested in seeing his friends and checking out the newest batch of female high school graduates than spending the time with his dad. Tom had thought about staying home, but it had been such a pleasant morning he had decided to at least attend the parade. It had been good to see Laura's dad faithfully in his position, walking, this year by himself with the other WWII veterans following in a car. It brought back good memories.

"You staying for the barbeque?" he asked Jim.

"I don't know. It's awfully hot in this uniform and I don't want to risk spilling barbeque sauce or baked beans on it. It seems more and more I end up wearing my meals rather than eating them."

"I don't know, Dad. That uniform is quite striking. Seems to me I can see a number of widows who would be only too happy to clean you up," Tom teased.

"And what about you? Where's that divorcee you were dating?"

"Just friends, now, remember."

"That's not what I hear, but then if that is the case, there are a number of fine looking women who would love to be more than friends with someone like you."

"All right, we're even. But I'm not looking."

"Neither am I. Last I need is a woman trying to run my life."

"Grandpa, did you want to go?" Joy found him.

"I don't know, honey, are you ready?"

"Well, I thought I might hang out with my friends, but I can take you home first if you want."

"Don't worry, Joy. I can take your grandpa home. You go enjoy your friends," Tom interrupted.

"Is that okay with you, Grandpa?" Joy asked.

"It's fine. You don't want us two old men cramping your style, besides you might cramp my style," Jim told her and sent her away.

The smell of barbeque chicken was already spreading throughout the park. What harm would there be in enjoying a good chicken barbeque with his son-in-law? He had to eat anyway.

Jim and Tom went to the barbeque tent and waited in line to get their chicken dinners, complete with baked beans, corn on the cob, coleslaw and watermelon. Even to his aging taste buds, it tasted great. Food always tasted better outside. He didn't know what it was that made it so, but it was so. Even the beans and K-rations they had had while in the army tasted better when eaten outside under the stars rather than in the mess tent. He would look at the stars and wonder if his Linda was looking at the same stars and dream of when he would see her again. Good dreams of a possible future. Those dreams had become a reality. Despite the difficulties they had endured, the reality had been better than the dreams, so much better.

But now it was but a dream once again, the reality of her having disappeared with her death, but the memory hadn't faded. The dream remained, but in a different form. Now when he looked

138

at the stars he saw her face among them and knew she was waiting for him.

"I'll be seeing you," he thought to himself as strains of this song from his war years echoed in his memory. He remembered the words so well. Better than what he had for breakfast. He remembered it every time he looked at the moon and thought of her. The melody replayed in his head. He dreamed of being with her again, but in the meantime he still had to live each day one day at a time. He needed something to do, to continue to give meaning to his life, rather than simply waiting for his death. But what could he do?

Maybe he could volunteer, maybe for the Red Cross. He couldn't give blood, but he could help at blood drives. Or maybe there was still something he could do for those young men and women serving now in Iraq. Maybe there was something he could do. He didn't know what. All of his life he had worked with his hands, in construction. Now that his hands no longer served him so well, certainly there was something more he could do. His thoughts wandered as he ate his meal.

Sure enough, his meal ended up on his uniform, barbeque stain in one spot, baked beans in another and pieces of corn and coleslaw in his lap.

"Hi, Grandpa," Tom's youngest son joined them along with some of his friends.

"I thought you were scoping out the new batch of female graduates," Tom said.

"Had to take a break to eat," Greg said. "Mind if we join you?" The table filled with young voices, talk of where they were going to school, what they were doing this summer and the latest movies and music. Jim only heard parts of the conversation, the buzz of so many voices drowning out the actual words. He was actually grateful to be left with his thoughts. It was nice to be surrounded by youth though.

"So what do you think, Grandpa?" Greg asked.

"Sorry, about what?" he replied.

"About Joe quitting school to join the army? His parents are dead set against it. He figures the war in Iraq is already over, worst that he'll see is some mopping up, assuming that's still going on by the time he enlists and completes his training. Then when he's finished the army will pay for his education. What do you think?"

"I think, best-laid plans of mice and men often go awry. I wouldn't sign on if I wasn't ready to fight. Who knows how much longer this might drag on, or where the next war will be? Doesn't sound like a good idea to me," Jim commented.

"That's what I tried to tell him," Greg said.

"I'm ready to fight," Joe said. "Having my education paid for is just a nice perk. I want to get Osama."

"Not going to get him in Iraq," Tom commented. Then a group of girls walked by and the conversation shifted as they quickly finished their meal to pursue better entertainment.

Jim began to realize just how tired he was.

"Ready to go home?" Tom asked.

"I believe I am. It was good eating with you. Now a nap sounds even better."

"Take it easy, Grandpa," Greg said as he prepared to leave with his friends.

"That was nice," Tom commented during the drive home. "I'm glad you stayed and ate with us."

"I didn't see anyone offering to take care of this old uniform. Seems I made a mess."

"Let me take it, Dad. I'll have it dry-cleaned. You okay?"

"Just tired," Jim said, "just tired. Just being around all of that young energy is enough to tire me out."

"I know what you mean. I wish I had some of their energy," Tom said as he dropped Jim off, staying just long enough to get his uniform.

It felt good to be home by himself, Jim thought. The day had been tiring, but also the conversation, as much as he enjoyed Tom and Greg's company. It reminded him once again of what he had lost, his daughter Laura, Tom's wife. His own wife. It was upsetting to hear Greg's friends talk of war. It was upsetting to think about Greg losing a friend in yet another war.

"Will we ever learn?" he asked himself. WWII had been different. Some compared Saddam to Hitler, but was he really that bad? Did he really need to be stopped? Weapons of mass destruction were supposedly hiding somewhere in Iraq. Was he bent on world domination? What had he done to us? He wasn't

140

Osama bin Laden, wasn't linked to Al Qaeda. In fact he had been an American ally not so long ago. It just didn't make a lot of sense to him.

"Bob, you didn't die in vain. You died for freedom, but there are other wars, this current war, did we really have just cause, just reason or is it only over oil? Will you think me disloyal or unpatriotic if I speak out about this war? It's in honor of your memory I do this, if I chose to do this. In honor of you and all those who died. You died so that others wouldn't have to die, and yet here we are in the middle of another war with more young men dying. . ." Jim thought long and hard. "At least I still have my brain," he told himself. "That much I do have."

"I need a dream, a new dream, something to make my life worthwhile, to give the time I have left meaning. A dream to carry me through this life and into the next. A dream of a better world. I can still make a difference," he thought as he picked up the flyer he had been given by the Veterans for Peace member. On it was listed the time, date and location for their next meeting. He marked it on his calendar.

The next day he picked up the phone and called the Red Cross and found out about volunteering there as well as calling Meals on Wheels to see if the program needed help with deliveries. Volunteering would keep him active and young he told himself. It would give him something to do besides waiting to die.

XV

"Mr. Peters, Mr. Peters, watch this! Watch me!" a chorus of students kept calling to him or running up to him to show him their ribbons, complain about unfairness or that someone was picking on them. It was a great day. Sunny with just enough clouds floating by to give a break from the sun. At one point it looked like rain might be threatening, but this was Michigan, the wind blew the clouds away with nary a drop being shed, except for sprinkles from students with water balloons or with water bottles trying to spray each other. Seventy degrees hot in the sun, cool in the shade. He cheered his class on in all the contests.

Field day. It wasn't meant to be a competition but fun, a chance to play some cooperative games, challenge the students physically while throwing in some learning in the process. Some of the games required some basic math, mostly it was fun. Despite efforts to keep competition to a minimum and make sure every student got a prize for something, they still couldn't make it through the day without some tears and broken hearts. Can you ever get three hundred-plus students together without there being tears? Not possible. Rare were the days when Kevin didn't have someone coming to him in tears from his twenty-two students, multiply that by five grade levels, first through fifth, three classes per grade, that was a lot of tears.

The kindergarten class didn't participate in field day but had its own closing picnic and this year the fifth graders had gone roller-skating, lessening the commotion. The fourth graders got a chance to see what it was like to be the oldest kids in the school in preparation for next year.

It was a fun day. Parent volunteers helped with the games and lunch, freeing him to enjoy a relaxing day as the school year was drawing to a close, perhaps his last year there.

"Are you coming back next year?" Asked the mother of one of his students.

"Don't know. I got a pink slip along with all the other teachers who had in less than ten years seniority. We won't know for sure till sometime this summer."

"Are you applying to other school districts?"

"Haven't really thought about it yet."

The pink slip had been expected. School budgets were tight everywhere. Routinely a number of the newer teachers would get a pink slip at the end of the school year. The union required advance notice before a teacher could be dismissed and so the administration would give out more pink slips than it thought absolutely necessary just so administrators wouldn't be forced into keeping on teachers if there was not enough money. Often, once administration knew who would be retiring and the budget was settled, all those who had received pink slips would be called back for the next year.

He wasn't overly worried, still it would take some time until it would all be worked out. Veteran teachers with seniority could count on a position within the school district, although not always the one they wanted. Other teachers without seniority but who had been through a number of years knew the routine so they didn't sweat it too much. It was the newbies, like him, who had to worry. Fortunately males willing to teach elementary students were in high demand so he hadn't been overly concerned about finding a new position if this one ended. He had begun the resume process last summer when he got called back for his second year.

This year he wasn't concerned either. In fact, the pink slip gave him a breather before having to make up his mind about whether to return to teaching. Thanks to Allyson's connections his book had been published and was doing surprisingly well. So well that the publisher wanted him to spend the summer promoting the book and was interested in a contract for another, perhaps a series. It seemed his alter ego, John Kennedy, mild-mannered science teacher, was a hit with middle-aged, love-lorn women, seeking a little adventure. Who'd have thought it? And this was a group with the money to buy his books. While not a James Bond or Sherlock Holmes, he also had some appeal to men as well.

So now he was faced with the question–continue teaching which he loved, or leave teaching for writing, something he also loved? Wasn't it possible to find some middle ground?

"No, dear, if you want to make it as a writer in this day, you have to be willing to promote yourself. That means book tours, speaking engagements. It's a full-time job, not something that can be done on evenings, weekends and summer vacation," or so he had been told. He hadn't really wanted an agent. That had been Allyson's idea.

"Why can't you take care of the contract, you're a lawyer?" he had asked.

"Because I don't know the business. You need someone who knows the ins and outs of royalties, copyright, promotion. That's not me. Give Judith a chance. I'm sure you'll love her. She's one of the best."

But he didn't love her. Already, under her hands, he could see his summer running away from him. Of course last summer he had worked as a driver's education instructor to supplement his income. Could this be worse than that he had wondered? Certainly this would be better but he had had visions of sleeping late, staying up late, going to baseball games, playing in a local league, going fishing, maybe writing, but all at a leisurely pace, not this breakneck speed, rushing from book signing to book signing.

"But the public will love you. You owe it to them," Judith insisted.

He wasn't sure he loved the public. He appreciated the fact that they read his novel, but he'd rather appreciate them from a distance, not this mass of middle-aged flesh, oooing over him like he was a baby doll, pressing the flesh, expecting handshakes or worse, hugs and kisses. It just wasn't him. And then there were the ones throwing themselves at him, middle-aged divorcees out for a fling. Out to get their fifteen minutes of fame through association with him.

He should have been happy. Someone else would have been happy. He was the envy of his friends.

"Fine, you go in my place," he told them.

Allyson was happy. Judith even more so. "You don't have to sleep with them. Just flirt with them a little, keep them interested so they'll want to buy your next book," she instructed.

But he wasn't happy.

"Kevin, what are you doing?" Allyson was surprised to see Kevin sitting in his office in a t-shirt and jeans holding a bolo bat, a small paddle with a rubber ball attached by a rubber string, hitting the ball back and forth, up and down.

"Shhh, I'm counting," he said as he missed. "Damn, I was up to two hundred. That's my record. Now I'll have to start again."

"But shouldn't you be packing? Aren't you supposed to be leaving on tour tonight?"

"Oh, that. No, I cancelled that."

"You cancelled that? But what about your career? What about your writing? Are you cancelling that too? What did Judith say?"

"Well she couldn't say too much because I fired her."

"You fired her. What will you do for an agent? Do you know how hard it is to get a good agent? To even get one to look at your work? Who will take you on after this gets out?"

"I guess I'm not worried about it," he said still batting the ball.

"What are you going to do all summer?"

"Now that is one thing I have figured out," he stated. She waited for him to continue. When he didn't say anything more she prompted him, "Well?"

"Well what?"

"What are you going to do all summer?"

"I'm going fishing, playing ball. I'm doing pretty much what I want to do."

"But you can't do that."

"Why not? Why can't I take the summer off?"

"But what about all of your plans? The book tours, the new book?"

"Oh, I might work on a new book, but then again maybe not."

"You don't even know if you have a job for the fall."

"I guess I'll worry about that when it happens. Don't worry. I'll pull my weight."

"No, it's not that, it's just . . ."

"What? Can't you stand to see me not work? Can't you stand to see me take it easy, take some time off? Can't you stand to see me happy?"

"No, that's not it."

"Then what?"

"I don't know. It's just all the plans, all gone just like that."

"Hey, they were your plans, not mine."

"No, they were our plans. I thought they were ours. I thought you wanted to write full-time. I thought it was your dream."

"Yeah, well maybe it was a nightmare. Maybe it wasn't what I wanted after all. Don't you want me to be happy?" His voice rose louder but he didn't yell. He wasn't going to yell, not like his dad. He was nothing like his dad, he told himself. He remained outwardly calm.

"Of course, that's all I ever wanted for you."

"Well, this will make me happy, trust me."

"Okay, I guess," Allyson acquiesced. She had no choice in the matter, but trust him, she didn't. She wondered what was going on. She wondered what if anything would make him happy.

Kevin really wasn't sure what he wanted to do. He just knew he didn't want to do another book tour and he didn't care if he never saw his agent again. Of course there was that lawsuit she was threatening for breach of contract. Allyson could handle that, couldn't she? Maybe if he just paid her off. He would still give her her portion of the royalties if she would just leave him alone … but any future books, whether there would be any future books, that he didn't know. If there were any he definitely wanted a new agent, one he picked out, not one Allyson found for him. If there would be any more books. That was one big if.

Perhaps he was just a one-hit wonder. Perhaps it had just been a flash in the pan. Perhaps the worst thing about these book tours and that other nonsense was that suddenly, he could no longer write. He didn't know what that was about. He just knew there was nothing inside of him to write any more. It was like the creativity had all dried up, drained out by that blood-sucker of an agent, he thought, trying to place blame.

Allyson wasn't much help either. Everything she tried to do for him just made it worse. He hated the pressure to perform, to be "on" all the time at these events he was supposed to attend. He hated the pressure to write. What had once been a fun pastime, had all of a sudden become a job. He didn't need another job. What he needed was some time off. That was why he packed his backpack the next morning and headed north to his uncle's cabin to go fishing. He left Allyson a note on the kitchen counter where she couldn't miss it.

"Gone fishing. Back when done. Kevin." No "love Kevin," no reassurance that he would call. Just five words and his name. It was the best he could do at the time.

Just five words and his name, Allyson thought as she crumbled the note. Is this goodbye then, she wondered. But no, his things were still here. Had it been that bad between them, she wondered. But no, it had been good until the last few months, until his book came out. Damn that book. "I wish he had never written it," she thought to herself.

The cabin was just the spot, a rustic place in the woods on the Pine River in northern Michigan. One room lit by a single bare light bulb hanging from the ceiling. There was but one outlet which was used to plug in a hot plate which was then used to boil coffee in the morning. Best damn coffee he ever had, Kevin thought to himself as he dropped his backpack on the floor and set what few provisions he had bought on the table. To listen to the radio the hot plate had to be unplugged.

Double-sized bunk beds lined the back of the room, large enough to sleep two to a bunk comfortably, three to a bunk uncomfortably. He remembered the canoe trip with his friends where they had crammed all six of them into the small cabin. By morning one of his buddies had ended up in a heap on the floor where he had fallen off of the bunk bed. He walked through cobwebs and knocked the remaining ones down with a sweep of the broom left in the corner. It felt like he was cleaning his head as he cleaned the cobwebs. He opened the one window to let in a little air and light, sat down at one of the two chairs at the table and began to think. What was he doing?

He threw his sleeping bag on the bed and set his backpack on the other chair. He put his provisions on the counter that served as cooking area and cleaning area. The sink was a simple plastic basin. He picked up the pitcher of water left by the last camper and the metal bucket and went to the pump. He primed the pump with water from the pitcher then pumped up and down until a rusty flow of water appeared. Must have been a long time since anyone used this cabin, he thought. Once the rust was gone he filled up the bucket and the pitcher, took them back into the cabin and covered them to protect his precious supply of water from bugs that inhabited the cabin.

Now to get down to the real business of this trip, he thought. He went back to his Chevy Geo and took out his rod and tackle box and the container of bait he had bought at one of the small store, gas stations that populated the lake region, popping up sporadically at any intersection. There was usually only one gas pump, used primarily for pumping gas for speed boats. The small store housed your basic essentials: toilet paper, milk, bread, eggs and an assortment of ice creams and candy for children, and of course bait for fishermen too busy to go out and dig up their own.

Even though it was broad daylight, the worst possible time for catching fish, he grabbed his supplies and headed down the steep, tree filled embankment, sliding on moss, watching out for poison ivy, until he reached the river. He eased himself along the bank until he found a good spot for sitting. Then baiting his hook and casting his line, he settled back, leaning against a tree, waiting for the fish to bite.

Now this is the life, he thought as he pulled his hat brim down to cover his face from the sun and closed his eyes. He could feel layers of tension easing out of his body as he relaxed for what seemed the first time in years, maybe since he had last come to the cabin.

There was something about driving north. No matter where else he drove, it just wasn't the same. Once he hit Clare, gateway to the north, the scenery changed, more woods, more pine trees lining the interstate and lakes. No more farmland, no more suburbia and shopping centers. The air smelt better, fresher, cleaner. Even when it smelled of campfires or burning leaves, it still smelled better.

He could feel his whole body shift once he got past Clare, but the real change didn't occur till he was out of his car, with the car unloaded, and he was sitting by the side of the river. The fishing pole was just an excuse to justify lying by the river all day. Years melted away, stress rolled off in layers deeper than he had ever imagined. When living with stress it became a normal part of life. You didn't even know how much stress you were under until it was gone. Sometimes the layers of stress and tension went so deep

148

it took days for them to finally release their hold on you; like peeling an onion, it took a while to peel away all of the layers and get to the heart. But what was under all the layers, what was in his heart? That was what he needed to know.

It was so peaceful by the river. He stopped only to fix himself a peanut butter sandwich before proceeding back to the river to eat. When he lost the shade in one spot and the sun got too hot, he pulled up his fishing pole and found another spot. He brushed off the bugs that were a part of any outdoor adventure and proceeded to snooze. Why did he wait so long to do this, he asked himself? Why did he have to wait till he was at a breaking point before taking care of himself, going away like this? He wondered what Allyson must be thinking about his note, but not too much. He pushed these thoughts out of his mind for now. These would be for another day. In fact, he instinctively knew his real problem wasn't with Allyson, but something else. Once he got the other taken care of, everything else would fall into place.

And so he spent day after day. Driving to the local store for supplies, drinking pot after pot of black coffee, eating the fish he caught during the day, waving to those who ventured down the river in canoes, keeping to himself, keeping his thoughts to himself as they sorted themselves out. He only needed time, peace and quiet and time.

She felt empty, dead inside. Tom had suggested she go to the Memorial Day Parade and picnic with him. It was always a big event. The whole community turned out for the parade, memorial service and barbeque afterwards, sponsored by the local Lions club. It was usually fun but Kate knew it wouldn't be fun this year. Too close to home. Frank's death made it all too real, what the day was about. It just plain hurt too much.

"It would be good for you, fresh air and sunshine. At least let me treat you to the barbeque." Tom had tried to persuade her but she knew better. Next year, maybe next year. This year she held her own memorial in the quiet of her home. So much had happened since last year around this time. Then she had been adjusting to letting Terri go away for the summer. She had only just met Tom, thought that Frank was dead. Now she knew he was. She had lived a lifetime in one year. Finding Frank, loving him, losing him. Letting Terri go, now accepting her back and then there was Tom. Where did Tom fit into this picture? It was all too much, too confusing. It hurt too much. She put him off and he backed off.

She was happy about Terri moving home, or she guessed she was, but she wasn't sure. Mustn't let myself get too happy lest she change her mind again, she had told herself. Terri had already changed her mind about the summer. She had the opportunity to be hostess at the Country Club. It would be good money, a good opportunity. There was no job waiting for her here so she might as well make some money while she could. But what if she changed her mind about moving home for her senior year as well? She could. Mustn't get my hopes up, Kate told herself. It hurts too much to have them dashed to pieces, like her hope for Frank. It just plain hurt too much.

She pulled out the last letter she had received from Frank and fingered it. She didn't bother to read it, knew it by memory. Short, to the point, Frank had never been one to waste words. Still it said all it needed to say.

Dearest Kate,

I know I have not been good at writing in the past. I apologize for that and for all of the missed opportunities throughout the years. I only hope that this letter is a start of making this up to you. I plan to spend the rest of my life making up for all of the missed time together.

I'm so grateful that you have come back into my life, so grateful for these last few months. I can't wait for this war to be over and for us to truly begin our life together. If anything should happen to prevent my return, I want you to know how much I love you, how happy I have been since you have come back into my life. I treasure the memories from the time we have had together and look forward to many more wonderful memories.

Love,
Frank

The letter had arrived the week after his funeral. Kate had stared at it, afraid to open it, afraid of what it might say, afraid of opening again the wound that was still so raw. When she finally

150

brought herself to open the letter she cried quietly as she read it. It had been dated the same day as his death. It must have been put in the mail that day, she thought. Since then it had become a source of comfort as she read and reread it, placing it in a safe spot in her desk.

It really wasn't as if they had known each other that long, and yet it had seemed like a lifetime. It wasn't just him who had died, part of her had died, her dreams for a new start, that part of her had died. And yet how real had those dreams been? Would she have really gone through with it? Were they simply straws grasped by an aging woman who wanted desperately to be young again, to feel young again, to feel life was worth living. A pathetic, middle-aged woman, that's all she was. Certainly Terri wouldn't have hesitated to tell her so if she were here, she who was so honest and so blunt.

"I miss that. I miss her honesty. It will be good to have her home, if she comes home, when she comes home, even if it's only for a visit. It will be good to see her."

Kate had kept her own personal vigil that night, lighting one candle and placing flowers on the mantel of the fireplace until the candle burned down and she fell asleep.

"What about starting your own practice? You could build an office with a separate entrance right at your home," Helen had suggested over lunch later that week.

"I don't know. I have thought about it, but haven't done too much about it. Preoccupied with other things, I guess. It might be nice to work with adults for a change, instead of teenagers. It would be a welcome change, but I don't know. There's the hassle with insurance and paperwork."

"Like you don't have paperwork now?!" Helen commented, knowing full well the stacks of paperwork on Kate's desk.

"Yeah, but this would be different."

"Precisely. That's one reason to do it."

"It might be nice being my own boss, not that Diane isn't great," Kate thought further.

"You don't have to quit your current job, just start to see clients on the side and see if there's a future in it for you."

"Maybe, but I don't want to work out of home. I think I'd like to keep that separate."

"Just a thought. You could hire that attractive contractor again, what was his name?"

"Tom." Kate thought back on how they had gotten to know each other. "How is Don doing?" she asked, changing the subject.

Too soon, it was still too soon to think about Tom, she told herself. But starting her own practice, that was something to think about. She wasn't getting any younger. Did she really have the energy to continue working with teenagers until she retired? It would be nice to have the flexible schedule of her own practice, but it was a risky venture. Now she had a guaranteed income, whereas dealing with clients she would have to work around their schedule to a certain extent and deal with insurance headaches as well. And then there were clients who didn't show, she knew that from past experience, from her small attempts at having her own practice. Now she was paid whether her teenagers showed up or not. Would it be worth it? She had thought about this before, had taken on a few clients, just hadn't really pursued it. Did she have what it takes to make it on her own? What would it hurt to give it a try? Maybe she could try again on a part-time basis and see if the practice grows.

On her way home from lunch she noticed a sign in front of a large old home that had been recently renovated. Office space available. She saw that the owner was an old acquaintance, the therapist she had seen while going through her divorce. She still saw her now and then at professional gatherings. She had been a mentor to her in the past, while getting her masters. Wouldn't it be great to share an office with her? That way she wouldn't be alone, like she would be working out of her home. She'd have other therapists to relate to on a regular basis. But rent an office? Too soon for that she told herself. She had to save her money for Terri's college expenses.

She dismissed the idea from her mind; still it remained in the background, taking on a life of its own. That life burst forth two weeks later when she ran into her former mentor while waiting to meet Helen for lunch.

"I see you have a new office."

"Yes, and I'm looking for tenants for the remaining offices in the house."

"It looks like a gorgeous building from outside."

"You should see the inside, beautiful woodwork, hardwood floors, open staircase, high ceilings. Stop by some time and I'll give you the grand tour."

"I'd love to."

"Here," she handed Kate her card, "Call me and we'll set a time."

"Maybe I will," Kate said, "maybe I will," she repeated to herself as she joined Helen for lunch.

To sleep, perchance to dream, Aye, there's the rub.
Hamlet

XVI

Back at their apartment, Allyson was left to pick up the pieces. Judith called, angry about his backing out on all of the speaking engagements she had arranged. She was threatening Kevin with breach of contract, but was willing to let this go as long as he agreed to keep her on as his agent for his next book. Allyson could only tell her she would do her best, would let Kevin know when, and if, he ever contacted her. She called his best friend from college to see if he knew where she could find him.

"Hey, Bud, it's Allyson. Have you heard anything from Kevin lately?" she asked.

"No, but then aren't you two living together?"

"We are, were, but he left a week ago, said he was going fishing. I haven't heard from him since."

"There was his uncle's cabin up north. I remember going there for the weekend once. He used to talk about it all the time. I bet that's where he went."

"Do you remember where it is?"

"Not really. It was pretty secluded, on the Pine River. That much I remember. No running water, no bathroom, just an outhouse. It did have electricity, though. Can't you reach him on his cell phone?"

"No. Look, if you hear from him would you let me know?"

"Sure, but don't worry. I'm sure he's okay. He used to do this when we were in college, slip off by himself now and then. He probably just needed some space."

"Sure, thanks," Allyson said. She had only called Kevin once, didn't want to seem too desperate, wanted to give him space.

"Hey, you okay? You sound like you could use some company," Bud asked. She assured him she was fine and ended the call.

It was a week before Kevin even checked his cell phone. He had turned it off once he got in the car and forgot about it. When he finally did check it, there were numerous messages from Judith.

154

"I thought I had fired her," he mumbled. There were several messages from his friends, including one from Bud. "Hey, dude, what are you doing? Allyson is really worried. Hey, are you dumping her? Cause if you are and it's okay, I would really like to ask her out. She is one fine woman. Anyway, call me."

There was only one call from Allyson. "Kevin, it's me. Just wondered where you are and if you are okay. Call me." He still didn't feel ready to talk to anyone from his "real" life, that part of him he had left behind. He just wasn't ready. He hadn't gotten to the heart yet of what was bothering him. He called their home phone during the day when he knew Allyson wouldn't be there to pick it up so he could leave a message.

"Hey, Allyson. Just wanted to let you know I'm okay. Don't worry about me. I'll call again sometime. Love you." He had hesitated before adding the "love you." He hadn't been sure that was the message he had wanted to leave, but now it was left, he couldn't take it back. It had just slipped out and now that he had said it, he knew it was true, but he still wasn't ready to leave.

Two weeks went by before he even knew it. He didn't know just what he was doing with his time. Little things like watching a spider build a web, checking out the squirrels that scampered across his roof during the day, chattering to each other, watching for hummingbirds and butterflies. The fourth of July came and went. He didn't miss the firecrackers or cherry bombs. Didn't miss the fireworks. He had stars at night and lightning crackling through the trees. That was enough for him.

Mid-July already. Time to start getting ready for the coming school year before he knew it. He still didn't know whether he had a job waiting for him. Perhaps a notice had been sent to his home, but he wasn't there to see it. Chances are Allyson would have called if she saw a letter from the school, maybe, or would she? He wondered how angry she was at him for leaving the way he had, but he didn't wonder enough to call, at least not just yet. Maybe she would call first, he thought.

He was enjoying the first real vacation he had had for years. Not since high school. Every summer during college had been filled with work to earn enough money to pay for his bills. Even during high school he had worked. He couldn't remember when he had had a whole summer off. He bathed by swimming in the cold, running water of the river, refreshing on a hot afternoon. He slept more soundly than he had for months, nary a nightmare to disturb his sleep.

He wondered why this was. Was it stress that had brought on the nightmares? And then, slowly, oh-so-slowly, after two weeks, he started to write again. He started to fill up the notebook he had brought with him. Nothing in particular, just writing, stories of his life in the woods. He wrote about the squirrel caught out in the middle of a thunderstorm, how it had curled its tail back over its head as if that small covering would protect it. He wrote about the two hummingbirds, battling over a single flower, zipping through the trees. He wrote about the fish he caught and the ones that got away. It was all for fun, nothing too serious. And he wrote about himself, his hopes and dreams and fears. He wondered, what did he want for the future, but he didn't write about that.

Finally after three weeks of silence, he called Allyson.

"Hey, Allyson."

"Hey to you too. How are you?"

"I'm fine."

"Where are you?"

"Up at my uncle's cabin on the Pine River."

"What are you doing?"

"Not a whole lot, fishing, writing. What about you?"

"Oh, you know the routine," she paused before asking. "Are you coming home soon?"

"I don't know."

"Are you ever coming home?" she asked softly.

There was a long pause as Kevin thought. "I wish I knew. I think so. I don't know. I hope you understand. I just needed to get away from everything for a while. I'll be coming home soon," he said and almost believed it.

"I miss you," Allyson said softly.

"I miss you, too," he replied. "I gotta go. I'll call again. I will. I promise," he said then ended the call.

Allyson didn't believe him. Neither did he.

And then the nightmare returned.

He was running. It was dark and he was running. He didn't know whether he was running away from or running to. He didn't know whether the fear that gripped him was fear of being caught or fear of losing something he desperately wanted, needed. Was he the chaser or the chased? If he was the chaser then he could stop, couldn't he, but would what he was chasing then be lost forever, for all time? If he was the one being chased and stopped he would be caught, but by what or whom? If only he knew. Maybe he wasn't being chased at all. Maybe it was all in his head. What was he running away from? What was he running after? What would happen if he stopped?

He was falling into some deep, dark pit, falling, falling into a well, a dry well with no end in sight. He could see above him, couldn't see below him, but at least he had stopped running.

"Boom!" Thunder cracked shaking the walls of the shack so that the walls continued to vibrate long after his ear drums had quieted down. Rain and wind hit against the wall, lightning brightened the outside momentarily, shining through chinks in the wood structure, under the door, through the window. It gave an eerie cast to the shack, which seemed to glow in the dark then receded into blackness. What was he dreaming about? Had it been the same dream again? If only he knew what he was running from then maybe he could face it, confront it and be done with it. But it was all blackness in his memory, no ghost illuminated the darkness.

His mind wandered back to his childhood. When did he first have this dream? Not as a child. He didn't remember waking up in the middle of the night as a child. He thought it started when he was ten or eleven or twelve. What had happened then? He had gone to middle school, a different school from grade school. He hadn't liked middle school. They had to change classes, the bigger kids made fun of him, laughed at him. Why? He couldn't remember.

He remembered his best friend had left, had been sent to another school. He had moved to another part of town and no longer lived in the same school district. He had felt lost without Mike. Mike had helped him. Mike had been bigger than him. No one picked on him when Mike was around. Mike made sure of that. But it wasn't bullies he was running from in his dream. It was something else.

He remembered Desert Storm. His dad had been in the National Guard. His unit had been called out. He remembered how proud he had been of his dad in his uniform whenever he had gone away to camp for training. How proud he had been when he left. How worried his mother had been.

"Don't worry, Mom. Dad will be okay," his brother had reassured her. "We'll take care of you," he had added.

Words of reassurance didn't help when the money just didn't stretch far enough. He remembered his mother sitting up with bills piled around her, crying and laying her head on the table.

"What are you doing up?" she said when she heard him moving about. "Get back to bed." Jack got a part-time job after school to help out. He had gotten a paper route. But the nightmares hadn't started then. It was when his dad came home from the war. That was when it started. They had all been so happy. None more so than he. Mom wouldn't have to worry anymore, he had thought. So they all had thought, but Dad wasn't the same. He wasn't the same man who had left.

Gone was the easy laughter that used to fill the house, how he and Mom used to dance at night when they thought he was in bed. His dad no longer wanted to coach their softball team or take them fishing. If he went fishing, it was alone. All he took besides his fishing gear was a six-pack and now at night he could hear his parents fight. That was when the nightmares began.

He didn't know what they were fighting about, couldn't understand the words. Then he heard a slap and his mom cry out, his dad slam the door followed by silence. The silence was worse than the fighting. Mom was downstairs at the kitchen table, quietly sobbing. Jack was next to her.

"Mom, you okay?" Kevin asked. When his mother looked up he could see the bruises on her face. Jack sent him away.

"Go back to bed, Kevin. I'll take care of Mom." When Kevin didn't move Jack yelled, "Get out of here, go back to bed I said." Kevin reluctantly went back upstairs.

"I'll kill him," he heard Jack say. "I'll kill him if he ever touches you again."

"No, Jack, he didn't mean it. He's your father. He's a good man. Don't say that." Kevin didn't hear any more as Jack shut the door to the kitchen. Not long after that his dad was gone.

He was running away from his dad, running away from home. How he longed to escape that home that was no longer home to him. When he couldn't physically escape, he escaped to his room, into his books, adventures, science fiction, mystery, anything that transported him out of his current situation. Other times he would make up stories and write. He dreamed of getting as far away from home as possible. When he graduated from high school he had picked a college far from home, making visits difficult if not impossible, UCLA, where he discovered he had some talent for writing, but not the confidence to say that was what he wanted to do. It was too precarious a profession. He wanted something he could count on, that's why he chose teaching. He wanted to teach little kids, wanted to go back to the time before the trouble began.

College had been fun. He gave his family hardly a thought except to wonder about how his mother was doing. But when it came time for getting a teaching position, he found himself drawn back to Michigan. Maybe it was the lakes and rivers, the woods, the seasons. He missed having four seasons. Whatever the reason, he came back. And so did the nightmares. Not right away, but after a while, after a year or so. He had been so busy at first, starting a new job, finding an apartment. And then he had met Allyson. Life couldn't have been better. He had been running so fast for so long, he even ran in his sleep, until it all came to a crashing halt.

"Boom!" Another crack of thunder. He heard trees cracking in the distance and prayed none come crashing down on his head.

What was he running from, he asked himself. Now that he was alone, he had finally slowed down to a standstill. There was no more time for running. What was he running from? What was he running after? Was he running away from his dad, away from the memory or running to him?

When he finally stopped running all that remained was emptiness. Was that what he was running from? Running from the emptiness within, emptiness where there should have been a person. He was not just running from his dad's anger, his parent's fighting. Perhaps what he was most afraid of wasn't his dad, but himself. What was he afraid he would find? That he was a fraud? A coward? Why hadn't he stood up to his dad, protected his mom like Jack had? Instead he hid behind his books, behind his brother, and now he was hiding behind the children in his classroom. He was hiding from his life by retreating to a safer time.

Time to grow up, he could hear a voice inside him say; was it his dad's voice? Or perhaps it was Jack's. Or someone else's? He wondered, was it time to stop running and face himself, embrace the darkness and in the darkness find himself?

Running from the loss of childhood. How he had wanted to return. Teaching children had given him a chance to return, but he wasn't a child any more. And yet he was still very much a child, afraid of the dark. What lurked in the dark but himself? He was running from himself, his loss of innocence, loss of childhood. But there was more. He wasn't just running away from. There was also someone he was running to. Allyson? He could see her face and he knew she was his saving grace. He had both been running from her and running to her, afraid to lose her, afraid to have her, just as he had been running from and running to himself. He didn't deserve her, didn't deserve all the good things he had, a job he loved, success as a writer. He didn't deserve it, they were all lies.

"What was the lie?" A voice echoed in his ear. He could hear his father's voice when he had won an award for writing a short story about a boy whose father had died in Desert Storm.

"You don't deserve this award. What do you know about war? What do you know about life? It's all lies. How dare you write about me this way?"

"It wasn't about you, Dad."

"You wish it was. You wish I had died, don't you. Then you could have your war-hero dad. I wish I had died, too. Get out of here you little shit. I wish I were dead."

His mother had taken him aside and said, "Don't listen to him, he's been drinking. He doesn't mean it. We are both proud of you." But he knew that was a lie, what his dad had said was the truth. He did want him dead right then, at that moment. And then, two weeks later, he was dead. Suicide. That was the darkness, the eternal darkness of death.

"What is the truth?" The voice echoed again.

I don't deserve to live, Kevin thought.

"No, that's not the truth."

I don't deserve to have love, to have the good things in life my father didn't have. I deserve to die.

"That is the lie. You deserve love. You deserve all the good that life has in store for you. You are a beloved child. That is the truth."

Allyson, Allyson, Kevin thought, as he lay there in the dark, her face present in his mind.

Had teaching both been a way of running away from himself and running to himself, he wondered. He had been trying to hide in childhood, fearing to embrace adulthood; yet through teaching small children he was called to be an adult. They, too, were saving graces in his life, calling him out of his own darkness and into relationship, one of responsibility and caring. And his writing? Had it too been a means of running away, hiding from harsh realities in fantasy, as well as a way to find himself? He needed all three. He had all three, but had he lost them? Had he thrown them away? Would Allyson take him back? Had he thrown away his future as a writer? And would there be a spot for him as a teacher?

He needed all three and somehow he had to get them back and find a way to balance them.

He didn't rush back home after this insight. He needed more time for it to slowly sink in, to separate the truth from the lies. He quieted that part of him that wanted to run back and catch Allyson, hold her tight to himself. That would scare her off. He needed to learn how to stop running, to sit in the quiet and the darkness and welcome himself. He no longer need fear the abyss for he had what he needed, knew what he needed, had confronted the darkness and come out on the other side. He slept, finally free from the nightmares that had been haunting him.

He had been gone over a month when he finally came home. He had been nervous about coming home. So much had changed and yet had anything changed? He had called Allyson and told her he was coming. He had been afraid she would tell him to pack his things and get out, but instead she tentatively, quietly, welcomed him.

"There's a letter from the school. I didn't know how to get it to you but since you said you'd be back soon I just kept it," she handed him a stack of mail with that letter on top. "You're going to have to deal with Judith, too. I put her off as long as I could. Now it's up to you to deal with her."

"Thank you. I'll call her tomorrow," he said as he took his mail.

"So, are you back for good or just a short while before you take off again?" she asked.

"For good, if you'll have me," he responded.

Tears welled up in her eyes as she turned away from him. "I guess we'll just have to see."

He was asked back to teach third grade again. "Eight more years and I'll have tenure," he told Allyson, "then I won't have to go through this every summer." He met with Judith and worked out an arrangement that both could live with. He may like writing, but he hated speaking engagements and book tours.

"Besides, I'll never be able to write another book if my time is taken up by that." She reluctantly agreed to back off, with the promise that she would continue as his agent for his next book, along with the promise that there would be a next book.

Kevin slept in the study for those first weeks back as he and Allyson got to know each other again, but it was okay, he was no longer running away. He was at peace with himself and Allyson could feel the difference. Now she felt more at peace being with him. And when he joined her in bed again, there were no more nightmares waking them both up and chasing him to the study. Together they slept through the night.

*We are such stuff as dreams are made of, and our little lives
are rounded with sleep.*
The Tempest

XVII

His life was full again. That life that had seemed so worthless, so
empty, was now full. Life was good again. He didn't know exactly
when it happened, but one day he woke up and realized he was
happy again. He was struck with guilt momentarily. How could he
be happy without her? But he knew Linda wouldn't have wanted
him to mourn forever. She would have wanted him to go on with
his life and at some point that is what he did. He made the choice
to live. The hole that had been left in his heart when she died was
still there, would always be there, along with all of the empty
spaces once filled by friends and family who were now gone. But
she wasn't truly gone. He knew that. Since God wasn't going to
take him, he had decided to make the most of what time was left
for him.

His life was full. Cataract surgery had given him his sight
back. He didn't like to drive at night, but he did take Meals on
Wheels to others less fortunate than him three times a week,
Monday, Wednesday and Friday. He had been active all his life
and wanted to stay active. He still had his Thursday morning
breakfast with friends and he now had a standing date for every
Saturday night to watch Lawrence Welk with the widow next door.
They also went to other senior activities together. It was
comfortable, a friendship Linda would have approved of, he was
sure.

He did go to a Veterans for Peace meeting but wasn't active
with the group. Instead he expressed his growing concern and
opposition to the war through writing letters to the editor of the
local paper. He also tried his hand at writing articles on his war
experience and experience with PTSD for magazines. He thought
perhaps his experiences would help others. And he was piecing
together some type of memoir, something to leave the grandkids.
Nothing fancy, just bits and pieces of his life, his life with their
grandmother, his life with their parents, his children. He wanted
them to have something to remember not only him but Linda,

Laura and Greg, their youngest, their baby. He wanted them to know who they came from, know their roots.

He had always thought Linda would have been the one to do this. She was the writer, not him. But now she was gone, the task fell to him. He turned the second bedroom into an office with his typewriter. There were pictures and papers, all sorts of memorabilia spread throughout the room. He had been talked into hooking up his son's old computer in the room as well.

"Dad, how are you going to keep up with the comings and goings of your grandchildren without email? It's replacing the letter. Also, you can do all types of research on it," he had been told.

And so now it sat unused in his office. His son had hooked it up for him, set up the Internet server and an email account but he had already forgotten how to use it. The best he could do was turn it on and play solitaire.

His grandson, Greg, had promised to come over during the summer while home from college and help him with it, but that had yet to happen. Jim much preferred working in his garden to sitting at a computer anyway.

"Hey, Grandpa," he was startled by Greg's approach. He remained on his knees, hands in the dirt. It took a lot of effort to get into this position and he didn't want to get out before finishing what he had started.

Greg came over closer to him, thinking he hadn't heard him. "Hi, Grandpa. I've come to help you with your computer."

"That's fine," he replied, "but first let me finish this weeding."

"Is there anything I can do?" Greg asked after waiting a few minutes.

"You can help me up," Jim said. It was always something of an effort to straighten up after working in the garden. Greg gave him a hand up and helped him straighten his legs and regain his balance.

"Thank you. Now I've just got to water these plants then we're done." He gently rained water from the hose onto the plants then turned off the hose, put away his garden tools and removed his gloves. Greg waited impatiently.

"You want some coffee?" Jim asked.

"No, I'm fine," Greg responded.

"Well, sit a spell while I get out of these dirty clothes."

Greg tapped his foot while Jim slowly changed his clothes.

"Grandpa, don't you remember? I called you last night to let you know I was coming."

"Oh, yeah, I guess I remember, but when had you said you'd be here?"

"Nine o'clock, remember. I have to be at work by eleven."

"Oh, I guess I forgot. Maybe we should do this another time."

"No, that's okay. I'm here." Greg realized that there was no hurrying his grandpa. He moved about as fast as he could and that was the best he could do.

"Now, did you say you wanted coffee?"

"No, thanks, Grandpa."

"Mind if I have some?"

"Grandpa, I don't have a lot of time."

"Oh, that's right. I keep forgetting. Okay, let's look at that computer." He led the way into his office. Greg wasn't sure where to start.

"You know how to turn it on?"

"Of course, I'm not an idiot."

"I didn't mean that . . ." Greg started then decided it was best to just let it go.

Jim turned on the computer and waited for it to boot up. "Pretty slow, huh, but fast enough for me," he commented.

"Okay, now do you know how to get to the Internet?" Greg leaned over his grandpa to check the connection. "See this, you click on this," Greg pointed to the dial up connection.

Jim tried clicking on but it didn't work.

"Double click Grandpa, like this," Greg showed him then clicked it off. "Try again."

Jim tried again and was successful. Slowly Greg walked Jim through the process, making sure his grandpa did everything himself. He checked his email, reading one Greg had sent him, and composed an email in reply. Then Greg showed him how to search for information.

"Let's say you want to know more about World War II. Just enter key words in here and click and voila," thousands of entries appeared.

"Now was that so bad?" Greg commented as they logged off.

"If only I remember how it works."

"Don't worry, Grandpa. It just takes practice. I'm going to send you an email again today. I want you to read it and send a response back to me. Try logging on again today while it's still fresh in your memory. That way it will be easier to remember."

Greg assured him that he would be back to check on his progress on Saturday.

"But what about your progress?"

"My progress? What are you talking about?"

"What about your progress with school, with life? How about we check your progress next time?"

Greg laughed, "All right, Grandpa. Next time we'll have that cup of coffee and talk about my progress, but there's really not much worth talking about."

"Oh, I'll be the judge of that."

Greg left. Jim took one look at his computer, waved his hand at it while shaking his head and left the room. Time for lunch anyway.

Greg returned on Saturday, true to his word. He had allotted more time so he wouldn't feel so pressed to get done and would be more patient. It was hard to give up a whole Saturday morning though, especially when you were young and had so much to do.

Once again Greg found his grandfather in the garden, but this time Jim was prepared for him.

"Good, I was just finishing. I like to pull the weeds before it gets too hot. I got coffee ready for us."

He slowly pulled himself up to a standing position, paused to gain his balance, then walked to the kitchen door.

"Help yourself to coffee while I get cleaned up."

"Okay, Grandpa," Greg poured a cup and sat down at the kitchen table, restlessly tapping his fingers. "Have you been going on the Internet like I showed you?" he yelled into the other room. "I haven't gotten any emails from you yet."

Jim walked back into the room, pulled out two pieces of pie from the refrigerator, placed them on the table and poured himself a cup of coffee. "We can talk about that after we've had our pie and coffee. See, Bess gave me an extra piece when I told her you were coming. Blueberry, fresh blueberries. Nothing quite like fresh blueberry pie for breakfast. Bess makes the best pie, I'll give her that much."

Greg settled back to enjoy his piece of pie. He knew there was no use trying to rush his grandpa.

"Grandpa?" Greg paused after his second bite of pie, "do you ever regret not becoming an architect?"

"Hell, no," Jim responded without hesitation. "I got to spend the majority of my adult life with the woman I loved. Had three great kids and now grandkids. What's to regret in that?"

"So if you had it to do over . . ."

"I'd do it all the same, except, I wish I had told your grandmother how much I loved her more often, your mother and uncles, too."

"She knew it. Even when she was angry with you, you could tell."

"So what about you? You settled on a major yet?"

"You know, Dad really wants me to go into construction with him. He doesn't say a lot, but I know that's what he's thinking. That's what everybody is thinking it seems. They all just expect it of me. My dad, my brothers, my dad's friends, the gang at work, even some of my friends think so."

"But what do you want?"

"I don't know. I do like to build things. It's actually been kind of fun working with Dad these past summers. I think it's just the fact that everybody expects it and I've always insisted I'd never do that."

"So what would happen if you did decide to go into the family business? There are worse places to work."

"Yeah, but everybody would say, 'I told you so,' or, 'see, I always knew you would do it.'"

"Everybody? I think you'd find the number would be smaller than that. And if they do, so what? It's your life, isn't it? You can do what you want. And even those few would most likely forget about that after a few weeks."

"I've been thinking maybe I could be an architect. I like drafting, coming up with designs."

"Company could always use a good architect."

"Or not. Always said I wanted out of this town, maybe move to a big city."

"It's up to you. You get your degree and you can go wherever you want to go."

Greg paused as he finished off his pie. "You know, my uncle Greg, the one I was named for, the one who died in the car accident when he was around my age? He had been going to go into the business with you, hadn't he?"

"Yes, he was. He lived to build. He had a knack for it. Was a great carpenter."

"Must have hurt real bad."

"Yes, it did. It's terrible to lose a child. I don't care how old they are. It was terrible to lose your mother. It was terrible to lose Greg because he was my son, not because he had been planning to go into business with me. Along came your dad, but even if he hadn't come along, someone would have. You're the third son, just like me. I didn't want to go into the family dairy business, so I struck out on my own. You can do whatever you want. Don't let others' expectations either force you into something you don't want, or keep you from what you want." He finished off his pie and put the plate in the sink. "You ready to do some surfing?" he asked.

"Sure, Grandpa," Greg laughed.

"You know," Jim said after getting up. "Building a life is a lot like constructing a building. You start out with a dream, a vision of what you want. Slowly that vision takes shape and you start to put it down on paper. As the process goes on, you realize that some of your ideas are just not possible. Goes against laws of physics maybe, or maybe they are possible but cost more than you can afford or more than you are willing to pay. So you make adjustments. You compromise here in order to get what you want somewhere else until you have your blueprints.

"Then you go into construction but even then it's not fixed. You might see an opportunity to do something different, better, and you go for it. You might get a good deal on some material and you take it. You might run into a problem that calls for more adjustments. But finally the building is done, you move in, walk around in it, make it your home, and, if well built, you're happy in it for maybe twenty years. Then it seems you are not as happy as you were. You've outgrown the space, your life has changed, circumstances are different so you want something different.

"Some people buy a whole new house. Others knock down a wall here or there, add on that master suite they've always wanted but couldn't afford, put in a sun roof to let in more light, change the kids' rec room into a den, whatever. They make changes to fit their life changes. What's important is to start with a big enough vision. Life has a way of whittling it down to size. You have to start big or you'll end up with nothing."

"And what happens when they hit your age, Grandpa?"

"Oh, then they move out entirely, are downsized until eventually, as Jesus says to Peter, someone ties a belt around you and takes you places you'd rather not go," he said with a smile.

"I didn't know you could quote Scripture."

"Lots you don't know about me. Now let's get to this computer thing."

"Don't worry, Grandpa. When I build my house, I'll make sure there's room for you."

"May I live to see that day!"

In the spring of '27, something bright and alien
flashed across the sky.
A young Minnesotan (Charles Lindbergh) who seemed to have
had nothing to do with his generation, did a heroic thing, and for a
moment people set down their glasses in country clubs and
speakeasies and thought of their old best dreams.
F. Scott Fitzgerald

XVIII

The year passed by quickly for Kate. It was good to have Terri home. She was seeing a few clients on a private basis, but her time was taken up with her job and Terri's senior year activities–exploring colleges, senior prom, graduation, graduation party–also her niece's upcoming wedding. So much to do to keep her occupied; so little time to grieve over what could have been. In her mind she wrote and rewrote letters to Frank, letters she wished she could deliver. She wrote in her journal, hoping, trusting Frank could read what was in her heart from his vantage point in heaven.

And then there was Tom.

They had not spoken much since that fateful trip to D.C. They would acknowledge each other when they passed on the street or saw each other in stores but nothing more. Tom had been giving her space; she had needed space, but it was hard to avoid each other for long.

"Hey," Tom said as they passed each other in the grocery store.

"Hi," Kate responded and prepared to continue down the aisle as had become their custom.

Tom placed his hand on her shopping cart. "You look good. How are you?"

"I'm okay. How about you?"

"Good, I'm good." There was an awkward pause till Kate broke the silence.

"That's good. Guess I better get going."

"You want to get coffee sometime?" Tom asked.

"Sure, when?"

"How about now?"

They went to the coffee shop in the store and sat down. Conversation was slow at first then picked up as they caught up on what each had been doing, ignoring what was left unspoken.

"So Terri's home?"

"Yes, senior year. Lot's going on."

"What about you? What's going on with you?"

"Not much, work, pretty much what I've been doing.

"Dating anyone?" Tom feigned disinterest as he drank his coffee.

"No, it's still too soon. What about you?"

"No one significant." Yet another awkward silence ensued. This time Tom broke the silence and said hesitantly, "Do you think you could ever care for me the way you cared for him?"

Kate looked away from him. "Do you think you could ever care for me the way you cared for Laura?"

"Touché," Tom responded, "I get the point."

"But maybe we could love each other in a different way."

"Maybe." They sat for a few minutes till Kate got up.

"I've got to go. Have to get these groceries home. It was good to see you," Kate said as she prepared to leave. "So, call me?"

"I will," Tom said and he did. That had been about six months ago. Since then he had become a regular part of her life, her family. It wasn't the same as with Frank, but it was good in a different way. And somehow she felt Frank would understand.

Tom had attended Terri's graduation with her, holding her hand as she cried. He had helped with all of the preparations for Terri's graduation party, picking up the cake, running to the store during the party to pick up ice when they ran out, helping with the rental chairs and tables and cleaning up afterwards. She didn't know what she would have done without him.

Terri's dad had come for the big event as well, with his wife and kids, but coming from so far away, there wasn't a lot he could do. Kate had leaned on Tom through this. They had scheduled the party for the same weekend as graduation so her dad didn't have to make a second trip from California.

And then there was the wedding just a few weeks later. A June wedding. Her niece had scheduled it for later in June so that her fiancé school teacher would be done with teaching for the summer and so it wouldn't interfere with Terri's graduation. Two big family parties in one month. She wondered how Tom put up with it, but he was holding up remarkably well. So far he hadn't been scared off by her family.

This year she had gone to the Memorial Day parade with Tom, part of his family tradition. It had been hard, and yet it was good for her to do this. She was pleased to see Tom's father-in-law still walking with the veterans as he has done for years. She was enjoying getting to know Tom's sons and their families. Life was good. And even better, Terri was planning on attending the local community college for her first two years of school.

"You know, if it's a matter of money, with your dad's help you can afford to go to most any of the colleges you are interested in attending. You don't have to worry about that," she had told Terri when Terri gave her the news.

"I know. I just would like to have a better idea of what I want to do before I commit to a four-year college. Besides, I was gone my junior year. I'd like to be home for a while."

"So it's not so bad here after all?"

"Not at all, Mom," Terri replied. "I'll have plenty of time to be on my own."

"This wouldn't happen to have anything to do with that young man from California you keep talking to?"

"Mom, we're just friends, although it will be nice to see him now and then once he transfers to Notre Dame."

The day of the wedding was here. They had had the rehearsal and rehearsal dinner last night. Terri was a bridesmaid. Tom was helping as an usher. All Kate had to do was show up, and maybe hold her sister's hand. The wedding was to be in the Methodist church in the small town where Allyson had grown up and where her parents still lived, just a forty-minute drive. Tom had come over that morning so they could drive together to Helen's home before the wedding to help with any last-minute details that needed attention. Terri had spent the night there with her cousins. Tom's cell phone rang as they were preparing to leave.

"Yeah, what happened?" Tom asked. Kate could hear the concern in his voice. "I'll be right over."

"What's the matter?"

"It's Jim, my father-in-law. Seems he was in his garden as usual this morning, working in the hot sun, then he passed out. His

172

neighbor called the ambulance. She called my home and got Greg. He went right over, beat the ambulance. Jim was sitting up by then and insisting he didn't need an ambulance. Finally Greg was able to talk him into going to the hospital. He's at the hospital right now."

"I'll go with you," Kate insisted.

"No, you've got the wedding. I'll go to the hospital and meet you later at the church."

"No, I want to go with you to make sure he's okay first. We can take separate cars so if I have to leave without you I can."

"Okay," Tom agreed rather than lose time arguing.

When they reached the hospital, Jim was sitting up in a bed in the emergency room, waiting to be admitted. Greg was with him as well as Bess, his neighbor.

"Getting awfully crowded in here," he grunted as they came in. "What are you all gussied up for?"

"Remember, Kate's niece is getting married today," Tom reminded him.

"Then why in God's name are you here?"

"I wanted to make sure you were okay."

"Do I look like I'm not okay? Why can't I convince anyone to let me out of here?"

"Grandpa, they just want to run some tests, make sure you didn't have a mini-stroke or anything," Greg interjected.

"Nothing wrong with me. I just got a little light-headed. Probably stayed out in the sun too long."

"You are a little dehydrated, that's why they are giving you fluids intravenously," Greg explained.

"I'm perfectly capable of drinking water on my own."

"Well, this will be quicker which means all the quicker you'll get out of here," Greg reassured him.

Jim grunted, realizing he might as well cooperate if he were ever going to get out of there. "The least they could do is get me a decent room with a TV. I don't want to miss the game this afternoon."

"They're working on it, Grandpa."

"What are you still doing here?" he asked Tom. "Don't you have a wedding to go to?"

"Well, yes. I wanted to make sure you were okay."

"Like I said, do I look not okay?"

"No, you look fine, just as ornery as ever," Tom said with a laugh.

"Don't worry, Dad. I'll stay with Grandpa. I'll call you if there are any problems."

"There is one thing you can do," Jim said before they left. "Why don't you take Bess here home?" Jim turned to Bess, "There's no reason for you to sit around here all day, Bess. Go on home. I'll be home in time for Lawrence Welk tonight."

"Well, all right," Bess reluctantly agreed. "But if not, I'll come back tonight to watch Lawrence with you."

"It's a date," Jim said.

Tom and Kate dropped Bess off then went to Helen's. They left Kate's car at the hospital. "Just in case he's still here when we get back," Tom had said.

The wedding went off with nary a hitch. The bride was escorted down the aisle by her father. The only evidence of his stroke was his cane and a slight limp. He had been working in therapy all year with this as his goal. Helen beamed. She was so happy. Kevin fumbled some, forgetting to repeat after the minister until poked by his best man. He wasn't having second thoughts. He had known since last summer that Allyson was the one for him. He just couldn't believe it was actually happening. It was all too good to be true. He hadn't seen a lot of Allyson these past few weeks. She had been so busy with wedding preparations. He had felt more like he was in the way than a help.

"All you need do is show up and bring the ring," his mother had told him. They had agreed to live separately for the month before the wedding to make the day more special. Kevin had thought it was a crazy idea but had agreed to go along with it. He had moved in with his old roommate while Allyson turned their apartment into the staging area for the wedding. It had actually been nice to get away. They were closing on a house which they planned to move into when they were back from their honeymoon. Kevin's second book had yet to materialize but between Allyson's job and his royalties from his first book they had been able to afford a honeymoon and the down payment on a home.

He had hardly seen Alyson this past week. He had been floored when she walked down the aisle in her wedding gown. Was it possible he could have forgotten how beautiful she was? Yet there she was and they were starting their life together. It just doesn't get better than this, he thought.

Jim was relieved to have the room cleared of visitors. Finally he felt like he could relax into the bed. No more putting on a good front for his loved ones.

"Tired, Grandpa?" Greg asked as he saw him lean back in the hospital bed and close his eyes.

"I'm just resting my eyes," he said.

"Well, hopefully you'll get a room soon. I'll see what's up," Greg went to the nurses' station.

Jim was glad for the moment of privacy. It had been a little frightening that morning. He had tried to stand up like he always did when his head had started to swim. Next thing he knew Bess was standing over him. Then came Greg and the paramedics. What a fuss they made when all he really needed was a glass of water and a chance to let the blood get back to his head. But instead he had been dragged off to this God-forsaken place on a stiff board.

And now they would probably run every test under the sun just to make sure. He knew from visiting friends in the hospital his age. Once they got you in they decide to check everything because at his age, who knew when they would get a chance again. He could die first, or at least die from the procedures. If that was what was about to happen, he didn't want it to happen here. He would have much rather have died in his garden, out in God's good earth, rather than in this sterile environment. But not this time. It wasn't his time yet.

It was afternoon before he was admitted to a room. They had already done some preliminary tests. It appeared he was out of any real danger so he had been assigned to a regular floor rather than ICU or CCU. Now it was just a matter of getting test results back and hearing from the various doctors, all of the specialists who got called in to look at every aspect of his anatomy: cardiology, neurology, pulmonary, the list went on. Greg stayed with him the whole time.

"Don't you have something better to do with your time?" Jim grunted.

"Nope, Grandpa, nothing more important than you."

"Well, let's see what's on TV." He flipped through the channels but it was too soon for the baseball game he wanted to watch. He ended up at one of the classic movie stations. "The Spirit of St. Louis," starring Jimmy Stewart was on.

"You've seen this before?" he asked his grandson.

"No, don't think I have."

"Jimmy Stewart is great. It's all about Charles Lindbergh's flight across the Atlantic to Paris. Lucky Lindy, certainly you know about that."

"I vaguely remember something, maybe . . ."

"What do they teach you kids? One of the greatest days in history. Bigger than the moon landing. I ought to know because I was around for both events. I was just a kid but I still remember it. It wasn't like it is today with TV cameras everywhere reporting minute by minute. All we had were our radios. It was as if the whole world were focused on this one man's heroic solo flight across the Atlantic. It was all everyone talked about.

"'You heard the latest?' they would ask and we all knew what they were referring to. 'Where is he now?' We prayed he would make it safely and when he successfully landed in Paris, the cheers went up around the country. He was a true hero, not one of those false heroes you see on reality shows today, all looking for their fifteen minutes of fame. No, he was a true hero. It was one of those moments you never forget. We talked about it for months afterwards." He paused before quoting, "People set down their glasses in country clubs and speakeasies and thought of their old best dreams."

"What's that from? More Scripture?"

"No, the Great Gatsby. What do they teach you young people?" he said then returned to the TV.

"The movie doesn't do him justice," Jim commented then drifted off to sleep, tired from the events of the day.

Greg quietly watched the movie while his grandpa slept.

"How's he doing?" Kate asked as Tom sat back down after going out to call Greg at the hospital.

"Just fine. He's watching Lawrence Welk with Bess. They're just keeping him overnight as a precaution."

"That's a relief," Kate stated. It had truly been a good day. Good to see her sister so relaxed, so happy. Good to see her brother-in-law doing so well. Good to see her niece and new nephew so happy, beginning their lives together. Good to have Terri home for now. Who knows what the future may bring, where she might travel, but for now she was home. And it was good to have a good man, a solid friend, by her side. Who knew what tomorrow would bring, what challenges to overcome, new joys as well as new sorrows? But for now, for tonight, there was the dance, dreams of yesterday, dreams of tomorrow, day after day until all of our dreams are yesterday, lost in this moment of time, lost in this dance called life.

Characters

Kate (Kathleen) Connors, formerly Jackson – social worker, 46 year old divorcee with sixteen-year old daughter, Terri.

Terri Connors – sixteen-year old daughter to Kate and Dick.

Dick Connors - lawyer, former husband to Kate, father of Terri, currently married with two step children, Alex and Alyssa.

Frank Shaughnessy – general, Kate's high school romance. Divorced with one son, Chad who is also in the military.

Chad Shaughnessy – son of Frank Shaughnessy, military officer.

Tom Jensen – building contractor, widower with three sons, youngest in college.

Greg Jensen – youngest son of Tom, currently in college.

Jim – World War II veteran, father-in-law to Tom Jensen, grandfather to Greg. Wife, Linda and daughter, Laura (Tom's wife), both died from cancer years ago.

Helen Peterson – Philosophy professor and candidate for political office, early 50's, married to Don, two adult daughters, Allyson and Lindsey.

Don Peterson – retired businessman, husband to Helen, father to Allyson and Lindsey.

Allyson Peterson – lawyer, daughter to Helen and Don, girlfriend to Kevin.

Kevin Peters – grade school teacher and writer, mid 20's, boyfriend to Allyson.

Josh Baxter – Terri's love interest.

Q&A on *Dreamweavers*

Q. What led you to write *Dreamweavers*?

A. I've long been fascinated by dreams. By this I mean waking dreams, dreams for ourselves, our future, our world, and how the dreams of our youth change as we age. In particular something happens in mid-life when we realize how far we have come from the dreams of our youth, how life has beaten down or altered our dreams. It is then that we need to find new dreams or maybe dust off old dreams that we have put aside, dreams more suited to our changing reality.

I found myself as I moved through my forties, doing what so many do, wondering about the one who got away, my former boyfriend. Thus Kate was born, an alter ego to live the life I would have liked to live. As the story developed I realized I wanted to have a variety of characters, all at different stages in life, all dealing with different aspects of dreams for the future. I considered sending Kate's daughter Terri away and thereby dismissing her from the story, but decided she brought an important perspective to the novel as a teenager just beginning to dream and create a life for herself. Because mid-life crises and how they force us to re-evaluate our lives and our dreams are so significant, I felt the story couldn't be carried entirely by one character so I created Helen, Kate's sister, to give a different slant on what may happen in mid-life.

I have long loved the quote by Oscar Wilde: "The gods have two ways to punish us – the first is to deny us our dreams, and the second is to grant them." I wanted a character for that quote. I also wanted to bring in more men, so I created Kevin, a twenty-something who gets everything he could have dreamed of but finds it isn't enough. Then to round out the cast of characters, I wanted someone in their eighties to represent the challenges of that generation when you have limited time left which then affects what you dream about.

Q. You mention the quote by Oscar Wilde. Where did you find the other quotes in your book?

A. I collect quotes. When I was preaching on a regular basis I would often find that the right quote would write half of my sermon. I had been collecting quotes on dreams long before I started writing *Dreamweavers*. In some ways, the quotes produced the book.

I had liked Langston Hughes poem on a dream deferred in youth, but it has only been as I've gotten older that I have come to truly appreciate its sentiments. What does happen to dreams that we keep putting off and putting off? Kate has put off following her own dreams while raising her daughter. Eventually these dreams catch up with her.

I'm a great fan of Shakespeare. *The Tempest* is a particular favorite with the quote, "We are such stuff as dreams are made on . . ." This is paired with quotes from Hamlet who is tormented with "bad dreams."

In my work with seniors where so many had seen their dreams crushed by failing health, I have been inspired by how they would find new dreams, new reasons to get up each morning and keep going, hence the quote from Joel on old men dreaming dreams. The final stanza of Mathew Arnold's poem "Dover Beach," is a serious look at the realities of war where so many dreams are broken.

I did not remember the quote from *The Great Gatsby* from reading it in my teens, but came upon it much later while a chaplain at a retirement community. I led a Memoir Group and remember distinctly a memoir one member had shared about Lucky Lindy and waiting to hear word about the Spirit of St. Louis. Her memoir had sparked similar memories within the group which brought home to me the significance of the event and the quote, "their old best dreams."

Q. So in some ways, the quotes gave birth to your characters and directed the action?

A. Yes, some of them anyway.

Q. What do you hope your readers will take away from your book?

A. To never stop dreaming, no matter what life dishes out and no matter how many times they are knocked down, to keep dreaming. And even more important, to keep loving. That's the message of the quote at the beginning of the book. In the end what matters is not our successes or what we have achieved but how much we have loved. *Dreamweavers* is meant to be a slice of life, two years in the life of this extended, inter-connected family. In the end what matters is love. So pick yourself up, keep dreaming, keep loving.

Note to the reader:

Did you enjoy reading this book? If so, please leave a review on Amazon. Your comments would be appreciated and mean so much to me in terms of helping others notice my book. You, the reader, have the power to make or break a book in this day of emarketing and social media.

Thank you so much for reading *Dreamweavers*. I hope you enjoyed it as much as I enjoyed writing it!

Patricia

www.ingramcontent.com/pod-product-compliance
Lightning Source LLC
Chambersburg PA
CBHW070954120726
47910CB00004B/1227